Rising from the Darkness

American Apocalypse

Book 4

By

AJ Newman

*

Acknowledgments

This book is dedicated to Patsy, my beautiful wife of thirty-four years, who assists with everything from Beta reading to censor duties. She enables me to write, golf, and enjoy my life with her and our mob of Shih Tzu's.

Thanks to David, Richard, and Wes who are Beta readers for this novel. They gave many suggestions that helped improve the cover and readability of my book.

Thanks to WMHCheryl at http://wmhcheryl.com/services-for-authors/ for the great proofreading.

Thanks again to the state of Oregon for being such an excellent setting for this story. I thoroughly enjoyed my research trip to Oregon to visit Bandon, Ashland, Medford, Grants Pass, and all of the bergs and land between them. That area is the setting for this story and several of my other novels.

AJ Newman

*

Published by Newalk LLC.

Owensboro, Kentucky

Chapter 1

Cole lay on the rooftop shuddering a bit due to the cold wind. He could smell the rancid smoke from a burning tire and heard the sounds of birds chirping as the sun's rays climbed above the snowcapped mountains in the east. Cole loved the early mornings before the rest of the world stirred for the day. He missed his family and Cloe but relished the solitude that the early morning brought each day.

He looked to his right and saw his friend and fellow sniper, Wes. Wes was much older and had retired from the Oregon State Police before the grid went down. Wes' best friend, Earl, and Wes had taught him a lot about military tactics, sniping, and fighting in general. Earl was a Marine and taught most of his friends how to fight to keep their community free. Cole felt very lucky to know these two warriors.

The man had a satchel on his side, and he traded a small package for two medium size boxes. The wind was blowing from the west at about three miles per hour, and the sun had not yet peeked over the mountains in the east. The rifle made a muffled report, and the bullet sped to its target. The unlucky drug dealer was 758 yards from the sniper's position, and the round hit the man on the right shoulder above the body armor on his side. The .762 bullet tore through the man and exited the opposite armhole in the body armor. He was dead before he hit the ground.

The drug addict attempted to take the satchel, but another bullet hit the bag as the man's hand reached for it. The addict looked up, and a bullet hit the man in the stomach. Wes had aimed for the punk's chest, but the man jerked upward when Cole missed him when he dropped to his knees to get the satchel. The man lay there begging someone to shoot him and put him out of his misery.

Cole and Wes scrambled down from the roof and Wes teased Cole. "Son you missed that druggie by a foot. Let's fetch that body armor and their weapons."

Unperturbed by Wes' taunting, Cole slid down from the roof. "Wes, that man dropped down like someone dropped a hundred dollar bill to grab that bag or I would have drilled him."

Cole liked Wes but didn't know him very well until they spent the last ten days together sniping and harassing the Boss's men in Medford. "I'm glad we decided to watch the drug trade as well as the Boss's enforcers and fighters. I always thought the poor drug addicts were innocent victims of the drug gangs. All of the ones we have shot have robbed and killed people to get things to trade for drugs."

Wes was impressed with Cole and was happy to help educate the boy as they accomplished their task in Medford. "Son, we've eliminated 9 of the Boss's men, 23 criminals, and 1 wife beater in the last 13 days. We also wounded another 12 of the Boss's men and suffered no severe wounds. I wonder how the other teams are doing."

Cole blushed then grinned. "You know darn well those other snipers aren't in our league. Let's go warm up some beans and spam then get some rest. I want to be in position on top of the Motel 6 across from that grocery store on Highway 5 as soon as possible."

Wes was amazed at how well this 16-year-old boy handled himself in these dangerous conditions. The boy had nerves of steel and was the best shot in the group. Cole was six feet tall and had dark hair. He had been a skinny beanpole type of guy six months ago, but the hard work chopping wood and other tasks that had to be done every day had bulked up his muscles. He now looked like a rugged outdoorsman with a dark tan and a short beard. Joe's daughter was Cole's girlfriend even though she was only 13-years-old. They were alike in many ways, and both were trained snipers for the group.

Wes was one of the men who brought his family out of Ashland to join Joe's motley crew of misfits from all walks of life. Wes was a retired Oregon State Trooper and was in his late fifties. He was just five feet six inches tall, but he was built like a linebacker. Wes had become one of the many staunch supporters of Joe Harp and his leadership of the group.

Over breakfast, Wes thought Cole had become very quiet the last few days and a bit careless. "Boy, are you missing that girl of yours?"

Cole's face flushed and felt hot. Wes was right. Cole missed Cloe so much his heart ached. Cole wiped his brow. "I miss her a lot, but it won't affect my job."

"Son, I miss Jill and my family, but you are all moon-eyed in love or maybe lust for your Cloe. Love is a good thing but keep your mind on business, or you could get us both killed. I know I tease you a lot about many things, but I'm not teasing now. Get your head back in the game."

Cole raged on the inside for a minute, but deep inside he knew Wes was right. Cole swallowed his pride. "Wes what you said pissed me off at first, but I know that you are right. I promise to do better starting now."

Several hours later Cole followed Wes through the abandoned subdivision behind the motel. Many of the houses had burned to the ground, and others had been vandalized. Cole thought he saw a face in a window every now and then and definitely saw a curtain move in one. He could tell which ones had the drug addicts and scum because you could smell them a mile away. They crapped out behind their houses with no regard to sanitation or their fellow man's wellbeing. They were the dregs of the earth.

Cole's skin began to crawl on the back of his neck. He heard a sound to his right. "Wes, we're being watched. I saw a face in a window on the last house, and a twig snapped behind us. Let's do the corner double back maneuver."

Wes grunted as they were even with the corner of the next house. "On my count. One...two...three."

Both men turned the corner with Wes standing with his gun aimed at the corner and Cole crouched with a knife in one hand and his 1911A1 in the other. They didn't know what to expect but were ready to fight. Cole kept glancing behind them to make sure there wasn't anyone sneaking up behind them. The wait was agony.

Just when they wondered if anything would happen, a head came around the corner. The head was attached to a little boy who was running for his life. Cole dropped his knife and caught the boy. "Whoa slow down. What are you running from?"

Unexpectedly two rough looking men in body armor and AR15s came running around the corner. Cole picked up his knife and thrust his blade upward into the man's groin slicing on into his lower stomach. The man's intestines fell out as the man dropped his rifle to try to hold his guts in his abdomen. The man looked down at Cole and bellowed, "You dun kilt me, boy."

Meanwhile, Wes butt stroked the other man and then kicked the man's legs out from under him. The man lay on the ground flat on his back looking up at the business end of Wes' M4.

Cole twisted around with his knife to confront the other man, but Wes had dealt with him. Cole bent over and wiped the blood and gore from his blade onto the dead man's shirt.

Wes saw the man he had pinned to the ground had all the markings of one of the Boss's men. "Why were you two chasing this boy?"

The man looked up at Wes. "The Boss will kill you for killing George. That is if I don't kill you first."

Wes pushed his rifle barrel into the man's groin. "We have two rifles aimed at you, and you are talking tough to us. I'm going to count to three and if you don't start talking my friend is going to cut something off you until you do talk. Cut his right little finger off."

Cole drew his knife and placed it against the man's hand. The man pleaded for his life. "I'll talk. The boy is the grandson of the Spirit. We need him to get the Spirit to surrender to the Boss."

Wes laughed and waved Cole back. "The Spirit is an urban legend. You're just talking shit to get us to let you live."

"No, ask the boy. We've been fighting the Spirit's men for over a month for control of North Medford. They keep hitting us with hit and run attacks and snipe our men from a mile away," the soon to be dead thug raged.

Wes drew his knife to cut the man's throat. "Cole, hide the boy's eyes. A young boy shouldn't see this."

The man rolled over quickly in a vain attempt to get to his feet and escape. He whipped a leg out, knocked Wes to the ground, and jumped to his feet. Cole calmly raised his rifle and shot the man in the stomach. "Wes, sorry for ruining your playtime, but I thought he might hurt you."

Wes sneered at Cole then patted him on the back. "I think that you are spending too much time with Earl, smart ass. I'd be mad, but you are right. I was overconfident."

Cole grinned at the man he respected. "That's why we make a great team. We make up for each other's flaws."

Just as Cole stopped speaking, the boy kicked Cole in the shin and tried to make a break for freedom. While Cole hopped on his other leg, he snatched the boy's collar and captured the urchin. "Why are you running from us? We saved you from those bad men." Cole asked.

The boy, who was about ten, replied, "Because my grandfather told me not to trust anyone outside our family."

Wes squatted down, examined the boy, and noticed that the boy was very clean and wearing nice clothes. This made him stand out these days after the lights went out. "Son, is the Spirit, your grandfather?"

Cole heard a noise coming from south of their position. "Wes, I think the Boss's men have us surrounded."

"No those are my uncles. Lay down your guns, and they won't shoot," the boy said.

Wes saw rifle barrels sticking from windows and poking around corners. "Cole, lay your guns down. They have a dozen guns pointed at us. Let's hope it's the boy's people."

They both lay their rifles and pistols on the ground and then watched four men walk toward them.

"Raise your hands. Who are you and why do you have one of our kids?" one of the men yelled.

Wes jutted his jaw out and focused on the man who just spoke. "We saved the boy from these two thugs. They were chasing him to use him for bait to catch the Spirit. We're from up in the mountains and are down here to stop the Boss from raiding our homes."

The man asked, "Are you the group that has been sniping the Boss's men and blowing up the Boss's buildings and vehicles? Wait, how did you get the M4s?"

Wes gulped and answered honestly. "Yes, we're part of that group. We have several teams in Ashland and Medford taking out the trash. We took the M4s from a gang that robbed the Medford Armory. The Mountain Men supply us with other arms and ammunition. If you join our group, you will receive training and enough arms to protect yourself."

Wes and Cole noticed that only one of the four men had an AR15 and the others had a mixture of lever and bolt action, deer rifles.

The man stepped forward and extended his hand. "I'm Carl, and I'm one of the Spirit's soldiers. It appears we have the same goal. What do you plan to do once the Boss and his men are all dead and burning in hell?"

Wes shook the man's hand. "We plan to go back in the mountains and mind our own business. One of our leaders will probably ask you to join our mutual assistance group. There won't be any pressure, but we have found there is strength in numbers."

"Are you part of the Mountain Men Survivalist Group?" Carl asked.

Wes could not tell from the man's tone of voice or facial expression if he felt the Mountain Men were good or bad guys. Wes braced for a response. "Yes, we have affiliated with them and are trying to get others to join our loosely joined group."

The man's disarming smile put Wes at ease. "We probably won't join your group, but we will want to be friends. Could you have your leader meet ours in three days? If you agree to meet, I'll be at the Motel 6 in the back at 2:30 pm in three days to take you two and your leader to meet our leader."

***

Joe steered quickly to miss a doe but managed to stay on the road. He gazed over to his wife, Cobie, and a smile came over his face. She was the light of his life and was strikingly beautiful with the sun shimmering on her raven black hair. Even without makeup or lipstick, the sight of her made shivers run up and down his spine. He was always amazed that such an attractive woman could be a stone cold killer when she had too. Cobie had saved his and her daughter's lives on several occasions.

Cobie's eyes opened. "What are you looking at Bub?"

"Heaven in a pair of dungarees and boots."

Cobie reached for his thigh and squeezed it. "I love you, Joe Harp. You make life worth living."

"Babe, I was just thinking the same."

Joe and Cobie traveled back over to Kevin's place along with Zeke's men who brought the promised supplies to Kevin's group. They arrived before noon and spent most of their time just getting to know Kevin and his family.

Before Joe went to bed, he read one of his Grandma's letters.

Dear Joe:

You know this damned medicine makes me a bit fuzzy headed every now and then. I hide these letters to make sure your aunt doesn't find them and put me in one of those padded cells. Well anyway, I had a good talk with my lawyer yesterday before my chemo treatments. He laughed his ass off about your aunt's inheritance and her family's treasure hunt.

Oh, shit, I just dropped all of the letters on the floor. They fell and went everywhere. I'll do my best to put them back in order but does it really matter because all of my letters have my wisdom and charm? That was a joke, Joe. I hope you're laughing and not saying to yourself. "Well, that explains the old bags incoherent letters that were out of sync."

It seems that it takes a day or so after each treatment to get me back on an even keel. My mind is still a bit fuzzy, but my thoughts are clear. I think.

Joe, I just reread this letter, and it makes no sense to me. Hey, have you seen Alfred yet? I hope you two get along. Take good care of him. Please.

I'll wait until tomorrow to write another letter.

Love Grandma

Cobie was asleep with her head on Joe's arm. He placed the letter on the nightstand and wrapped his other arm around his wife. Her hair smelled like Lilacs and tickled his chin as he nuzzled against her neck. Cobie's body was always warm and inviting, but her feet were as cold as ice. She wore Joe's heavy woolen socks every night when she went to bed. It only took a couple of times for Joe to think of the socks when she stuck her cold feet against his body. Joe fell asleep thinking about the old adage, "Cold feet and warm heart." Well, he knew that Cobie had the warmest heart and the damnedest cold feet.

Cobie woke to several strange but somewhat familiar smells. She quickly eliminated Joe's manly odors and the shampoo he had used to wash his unruly hair. She knew the potent smell of the coffee brewing but was giddy with glee when she decided it was the smell of bacon that wafted down the hallway from the kitchen to their bedroom.

Cobie spooned against Joe's back but didn't want to wake him since it was only 4:30. She felt she should be up helping Kevin's wife prepare their breakfast but mainly wanted to steal a piece of the bacon. She had not tasted bacon since the lights went out and the smell made her mouth water in anticipation. She slowly pulled away from Joe and rolled her legs off the bed to avoid jostling Joe. Before she could stand up Joe's arm wrapped around her waist and drew her back into the bed. He smothered her in kisses as he slid her T-shirt over her head.

Half an hour later Cobie and Joe lay there as madly in love as they were the first day Joe gave her the massage by the fire in his cabin. Cobie kissed his cheek. "Darling I need to go to the kitchen and help fix breakfast."

"Babe, I thought you said that you could live on love when we were married."

"Hon, I lied. I smell bacon, and I have to have me some bacon," Cobie said as she jumped off the bed.

The kitchen was very busy with Kevin's wife and daughter working together in the small kitchen. Cobie noticed they were both in housecoats while she was dressed for war with her boots and pistol belt not to mention her boot knife and a backup pistol on her ankle. She watched the women for a minute and thought she must be dreaming because this was a scene from before TSHTF. They were happy and talking about kids, grandkids, and the kid's homework.

Cobie wanted to catch the ladies attention but not scare them. "Good morning ladies. What can I do to help prepare breakfast? I'm a little late joining the party."

Kevin's wife insisted, "You are our guest. Here let me pour you a cup of coffee. You just sit there and keep us company until those lazy menfolk come to breakfast."

Cobie watched one of the ladies frying several pounds of thick sliced bacon and her mouth watered. "Do you make your own bacon? That smells heavenly."

The lady picked up a piece of bacon with a fork and handed it to Cobie. "I'm sorry. We have been prepping and living off the grid so long that we think everyone has what we have. Enjoy."

The bacon was crisp and had a slightly salty taste as Cobie's mouth relished the flavor. "We have started raising pigs but don't have enough to slaughter one yet. We hope to trade for pigs if we ever find someone with extra piglets. This bacon is wonderful. It's surprising what you miss until you don't have it anymore."

Kevin stood behind Cobie. "What would you trade for some piglets if we knew where some could be found?"

Startled, Cobie snapped around to see Kevin, their host. "Joe would have to answer that. I'm just a cook and female warrior."

Joe walked down the hallway toward them when he heard his name. "What do I need to answer? Can I have a piece of bacon? I'll trade anything you want for a bite of bacon. Well, almost anything."

A piece of bacon was offered to Joe, and he squealed with delight as he savored the treat. "Yes, we need pigs. What do you need that you don't already have?"

"We need bullets, medicine, a doctor, whiskey, beer, and someone who can gunsmith," Kevin replied.

Joe scratched his ear. "We have some extra bullets depending on what caliber you need. We also have a doctor, nurses, and a gunsmith. We can trade you their labor for piglets."

Cobie was a bit shy but spoke up. "I think the Mountain Men may have some extra medical supplies. I'll ask if they want to trade any of them."

Kevin's wife took a large bowl of scrambled eggs to the table. "Breakfast is ready. Sally, please feed the kids at the kitchen table so the adults will have some peace in the dining room."

The breakfast was only an average meal for these new friends; however, it was a feast for Joe and Cobie. Scrambled and fried eggs, bacon, fried ham, and toast and jelly were served. Just the smell of the different foods was a sheer pleasure for them, and Cobie couldn't wait until they could make their own bacon.

Cobie cleaned her plate and had two more pieces of bacon. "If I stayed around this place I wouldn't be able to zip up my pants after a month. Thanks so much for the fantastic meal. You all have to visit us one day and let me prepare a meal for you. We don't have bacon, but I make some flaky biscuits and mouthwatering gravy."

Kevin swallowed a mouthful of toast and coughed. "What caliber are your extra bullets?"

"We have extra .45ACP, 7.62 NATO, and some 30.06 bullets we can spare," Joe replied.

Kevin looked at Joe trying to read his face. "We could use all of the 7.62 you can spare and some 30.06, but we don't have any guns chambered for .45 ACP. Well, that's not true we have a couple, but they need some parts we don't have."

"Our man Earl can probably fix your pistols. Are they 1911A1s?"

"Yes, both were used by my great uncle in WWII," Kevin replied.

Joe laughed and tugged at his chin. "Then I know Earl can fix them. Would you like to have a couple of more 1911s?"

"Hell yes. I'll trade three piglets for one .45. I'll trade one piglet for 25 bullets," Kevin enthusiastically answered.

Joe pressed his luck. "Would you be interested in an M3 Sub Machine Gun?"

"Damn, you got one of those beasts. They'll clear a room in a heartbeat. I'll trade you a young sow for one M3 and two hundred rounds of .45 ACP. What do you want for the other bullets?"

They dickered for another hour and arrived at several mutually beneficial trades. More importantly, they set up trading meets every first and third Wednesdays each month to trade. They would do this for several months and then set up a joint trade day once a month for all of the groups to meet together and trade. Joe wanted to wait for 3-4 months for the large trade meeting to give them time to wipe out the Boss and his men.

Kevin slapped his hand on the table. "Ladies we are going to change the discussion to planning our fight against the Boss and Ashland."

All of the ladies left the room to go to the kitchen or to tend to their children. Only Cobie stayed behind for the meeting with Kevin, Joe, and two of Kevin's men.

Kevin frowned and waved to catch Cobie's attention. "Don't be bashful. You can join the women."

Joe almost choked on his coffee as Cobie's head snapped toward Kevin. "No, I need to keep an eye on this testosterone filled room and make sure we have a solid plan that won't get all of you killed. Let's get started before we all grow old."

Kevin looked at Joe for help, but Joe shook his head. "Men, our women not only train to fight as your women do, but they also fight along with us. Cobie killed a dozen men and a few women during the past few months, and she was tutored by our best trainer in tactics. Earl takes pleasure in making everyone's life miserable during training. My wife stood up to him and can dish it out with the best."

Kevin's face turned red then he grinned. "My apologies ma'am for thinking you were not interested. Let's get on with the meeting."

To Kevin's surprise, Cobie contributed as much or more than any of the men. Kevin asked Cobie to come back with Earl and help him put a more aggressive training program together for his group's women.

"Kevin, how many fighters will you be able to spare when we take the fight to the Boss in Medford and Ashland? Joe asked.

Kevin performed some mental math. "Twenty to twenty-five and we can still protect our homes."

Joe was pleasantly surprised. "That gives us 60 fighters to add to what Zeke can commit. I have to press him on that

16

this week. I think we will start a campaign in about two to three weeks. Do you have any trained snipers?"

Kevin nodded then grinned. "My brother-in-law is a Marine sniper. He has six fully trained and a dozen more in training. We could use some more sniper rifles. The new snipers are using bolt action Savage .308 and .338 Lapuas."

The meeting was almost over when Joe's radio beeped, and he had to step out of the room to answer.

"Joe, this is Ben. Come in Joe."

"Ben, this is Joe. What can I do for you?"

"Joe, we need you to come home today. There hasn't been anything bad happen, but rather a huge opportunity has arisen, and only you can handle it," Ben said.

Joe's interest was piqued. "I'll leave after dark, and you know how long it will take me to get home."

Joe walked back into the meeting to see Cobie verbally fencing with Kevin about how to raise rabbits. "Cobie, have you taught him all we know about raising bunnies?"

Cobie nodded and flipped her hair. "These guys don't raise rabbits. We're trading them several breeding pairs to get them started. They liked my story about me being sick and tired of rabbit meat. Kevin, we'll even bring my daughter over here to train your head bunny wrangler on the fine art of managing your Bunny Ranch."

Kevin chuckled. "And I told her that we're tired of pork and chicken."

Joe walked over to Cobie and whispered to her that they needed to get back home quickly and added that there was no bad news. He then addressed the others. "I'm sorry but something has come up back home, and we can't stay overnight as planned. I think we covered all of the business,

17

and we will return at the earliest convenient time. My apologies."

"Nothing too serious I hope," Kevin inquired.

"No Kevin, not at all. More of an opportunity. I'd tell you more, but we learned a while back that our enemies monitor the radio waves, so we don't give out any details over the air. The bottom line is you now know about as much as I do about why we're going home. Stay safe and give me a heads up when the teams filter back home," Joe requested.

They had only been on the road for a few minutes when curiosity got the best of Cobie. "Joe, you can give me the full story now. Is anyone hurt?"

"Babe, all I know is that there is no bad news and I have to be home to handle an opportunity."

Cobie was anxious to know what was so important that it would take her away from bacon.

They chatted about their short visit with Kevin and his family all of the way home. Cobie laid her head on Joe's shoulder and kissed his neck. "Hon, thanks for the support when Kevin was surprised that I was going to stay for the meeting. That means a lot to me."

Joe patted her on her thigh and returned a quick kiss. "Babe, I'll be glad when no one is surprised that women and young adults can fight as well as men. We know that everyone doesn't have the same physical strength, but everyone can throw a knife or pull a trigger."

Cobie giggled for a moment. "Hon, as long as women need someone to take jar lids off and the electricity is down, men will always be needed."

Joe switched seats with Cobie, and she drove the last half of the trip home. Joe was behind several weeks of his Grandma's letters and wanted to get caught back up. Their lives were moving so fast with organizing the people around them to fight the tyranny and to survive each day, that they had little free time.

Dear Joe:

I made sure this letter followed the last one, or you might think I dipped into your uncle's marijuana. Even though the letter didn't make much sense to me, I left it in the pile because it is a gift to you and I want to share the good and bad with you.

From now on, I will only write letters two days after my treatments. Since they are on Mondays, I will write Wednesday through Sunday. Today is Wednesday and that idiot Speaker of the House was on TV telling us that the North Koreans and Chinese are our friends and only talk tough because the President threatened more sanctions. I think the bastards will nuke us any day. Joe, I tried to call you at home today and got a busy signal. Doesn't your cell phone have voice messaging? I wanted to beg you to start prepping. I will keep trying.

I did reach your dad, and he has increased his preparation for the upcoming TEOTWAWKI. He told me that he actually has your mom helping. I thought hell would freeze over before she would become a prepper. I guess the bad news scared the crap out of her and she has finally seen the light.

Now if I can just get you to take politics seriously. Ambivalence might get you killed one day. The North Koreans have been perfecting EMP nukes according to the NSA and CIA reports that FOX news shared, but the other stations are talking about Singing with the Stars and Miley Cyrus's ass or tits hanging out of her whatever she is wearing today. That broad is a grandmother. What the hell is she doing showing her ass on TV? She has no shame, and no amount of plastic surgery will make that face look good again. If you stuck a pin in her face, it would pop like a balloon.

Yeah, that was major rambling, but I was of sound mind and enjoyed every bit of it. I'll try again tomorrow to call you.

Love Grandma

☆

Chapter 2

A few hours later, Cobie pulled up to their cabin and saw Cloe on the deck lying beside Cole in the hammock. Bennie was lying below the hammock keeping guard. They were locked in an embrace, and an earthquake wouldn't get their attention. Cobie watched for a few minutes and only saw them kissing and no grab ass, so she walked into the cabin with Joe.

They were scarcely in the front door when the kitchen door slammed, and Cloe came running up to her mom and hugged her and then Joe. "Mom, Dad, you are back early."

Cole's flushed face and guilty look gave him away. "I'm glad to see you two made it back safely. Joe, we were just lying there and weren't doing anything wrong. I promise."

Cobie walked up to Cole and hugged him. "I know, we watched you for a few minutes when we arrived. You also know that as much as I love you, I'll bury you in a nice grave if you hurt Cloe."

Cloe's heart raced as she put her arms around Cole. "Mom you do know that we could hear the Jeep coming up the mountain five minutes before you arrived. Cole was trying to get out of the hammock, and I held him to keep him from jumping off the hammock. The big chicken is afraid of you."

Cobie affectionately embraced Cole. "Cole knows I love him and would never hurt him unless he hurt my baby girl."

Joe moved closer to Cole and put his arm over Cole's shoulder. "Damn, you've grown another inch since we last saw you. Why are you back here three days early? Does it have anything to do with the reason we're back early?"

Cole breathed a sigh of relief. "Yes, Wes and I saved a young boy from the Boss's men and the boy turned out to be the grandson of that religious leader they call the Spirit. Some of the leader's men were following the men who took the boy and captured us a few minutes after we saved the kid. They want to meet our leader."

Cole finished the story, gave Joe the details of the upcoming meeting, and then discussed their sniping mission. "Joe we had a very successful trip to Medford. Wes will give you a list of accomplishments, but I can say that over two dozen are dead or wounded and won't be terrorizing the good citizens of Medford and Ashland anymore."

"Cole, I know you were only with the men for a few minutes but tell me about their arms and level of professionalism and military training," Joe said.

Cole looked down for a minute. "Only one appeared to have military training. He was the leader of this small group. They only had one AR15, and only two magazine fed pistols. One man had one of those hog leg .44 Magnums strapped to his leg. The leader had men all around us in the shadows, but their rifle barrels were mainly what you'd expect to see deer hunting. That's about all I remember."

Joe looked at the young man and was proud to have him as a friend. Cole was only 16, but Joe counted on him to perform a man's work and fight beside him. He took Cole out on the deck for a private conversation. "Cole, I'm going to ask Wes to head up a group to potentially stay and advise this group. I want you to partner with Wes and a few others to see what they need to defeat the Boss. We can't always be the ones doing all of the fighting. I'll ask this Spirit guy to join the Mountain Men and if he agrees the mountain men will help arm and train the Spirit's men."

"Joe, I'll do whatever is best for the group. Just tell me what my job is, and I'll get it done," Cole voiced.

"You'll be away from Cloe for another couple of weeks or longer, but Cole I trust you and your judgment. You are very important to me, and I will be using you more and more to help me protect our community," Joe said.

The expression on Cole's face soured, but he forced a grin. "That's a small sacrifice if it means I can make our group safer and Cloe's life safer. Now is the time while we're both young to get all of these horrible issues taken care of so we can lead a better life."

Joe shook Cole's hand and chest-bumped him. "Son, you will make a great husband and one day a great father. You are right about now is the time to strike. We'll meet with the others after dinner and put a plan together. Now let's eat and then you need to spend some time with Cloe and your parents. Remember you have a momma that is worried sick about you."

"Oh darn, I'll tell Cloe I'm going home for lunch. Where will we meet with the others?"

Joe thought for a second. "Let's meet at the bunker so we can see what Earl's team has accomplished. Tell everyone up your way. Let's meet after dinner."

'Dad, that was mean sending Cole home. I missed him very much," Cloe whined.

Joe took Cloe's hand. "I know you missed him, and he told me how much he missed you. I didn't send him off. He remembered that his mom and Ben were worried about him also and went home to visit with them before our meeting this afternoon. Cole will spend most of the next two-three days with you, and then he and several others will be back out in the field for several weeks.

Cloe, Cole and you have serious responsibilities, and sometimes they will take you away from each other. I know that you are only thirteen going on twenty-five and keep reminding us you want to be treated as an adult. Tough decisions and tough tasks are part of being an adult. What Cole does to help us rid this area of our enemies now will make it much safer for all of us including you and your future children. Sorry about the lecture."

Cloe had tears in her eyes as she hugged Joe, "Dad I know, but I miss him so much when he's gone. Bennie is good company, but I need my boyfriend around. I'll keep my thoughts to myself and encourage Cole to keep up the fight and spend as much time with him as possible between assignments. I'll also try to share him with Jane and Ben."

Cobie joined them in a group hug. "Baby, I miss Joe if he's gone from me for a few hours. I know how you feel, but the separation will be well worth the life you and Cole make together in the furure. Now let's eat so we won't be late for the meeting."

Cloe washed the dishes while Cobie and Joe unloaded the Jeep from their trip. Cobie tapped Joe on the shoulder. "Babe, how long will it take to make this place safe?"

Joe rubbed his neck. "Babe, anything is possible, but this will take time. We have to wipe out the Boss and his team, deal with the Muslim terrorists, and eliminate all of the gangs and criminals. The first two I hope we'll eliminate this year. The last one will be an ongoing fight for years. Hell, when the USA still existed, there were criminals, drug pushers, and pedophiles in every city. It will become easier, but I'm afraid we won't get rid of all of them in our lifetime. The big difference now is we can deal with the thugs as we catch them.

Thieves, murderers, pedophiles, and rapists will be executed when they are caught. No jail time for criminals."

"Would you kill a man for stealing? Cobie asked.

Joe clenched his fists and dropped his backpack. "Yes, I would put to death any adult who steals food or any supplies necessary for survival. Theft could result in an innocent person dying. Of course, we'll have to figure out how to handle petty theft and kids who take things that don't belong to themselves."

Cobie kissed Joe. "Hon, thanks for sending Cole on that mission. We need to cool off that relationship without being dictators."

"Babe, I'm glad you see it that way. Cole will be ready to have a serious relationship in a couple of years, but Cloe is still too young even though she's mature in many ways."

***

Cole dropped his gear, kissed his mom, and hugged Ben. They ate lunch and all Cole could talk about was how he missed Cloe and his recent mission. Cole was only there for an hour before running back to see Cloe.

Jane understood but felt slighted. She repressed her tears. "Ben, my son is growing up and needs Cloe more than me now. Oh, darn. You don't think they have ..."

"Hon stop. You raised a good man, and he won't do anything to hurt Cloe," Ben confided.

Jane leaned toward Ben and kissed him. "I don't think hurting her was what I was thinking. I love Cloe, but we have to remember that is a twenty-year-old woman locked up in that thirteen-year-old body."

Ben almost choked and ventured, "I hate to add to your apprehension, but that girl looks like a twenty-five-year-old. Have you had the talk with Cole?"

"Yes, and Cobie had the talk with Cloe. I'm just concerned what they will do since he's been gone for weeks and they will be all alone several times this week before he goes on the next mission."

"Darling, you can't keep Cole tied to your apron strings. You raised him right, and he will keep his wits about himself. Stop worrying. They are good kids. Hell I mean good young adults," Ben gently said.

Later about supper time Cole came back home and Jane met him at the door. "Hon is everything okay? We didn't expect you back for a while."

Cole looked at the tears in his mom's eyes. "Mom, I missed you and wanted to see how you and my family are doing. I'm sorry I ran down to Cloe's so fast after lunch. I missed her so much over the time I was gone. Mom, I also missed you, Charlie, and Ben."

Jane prepared supper while Cole filled Ben and Charlie in on the results of Wes and his sniping in Medford. Cole suddenly exclaimed, "I almost forgot to tell you that we have a meeting at the bunker in about an hour and a half. I stopped and told Wes and Earl on the way here. We will be putting a plan together on how to work with the Spirit's men in Medford."

"So this Spirit actually exists?" Ben commented.

Cole shrugged. "I don't know for sure, but those men acted as if he does exist."

"Mom, thanks for a great home-cooked meal. Wes and I have been eating cold beans, MREs, and whatever we could find. This is very good."

Jane was happy that she had all of her family back together. "Cole, I'm glad you came back to be with us. We all missed you. Even Charlie missed you picking on him."

Cole knew she wouldn't be happy when she heard about his next assignment. They finished eating and left to go to the bunker.

***

Cole and Wes had already filled in all of the others on the results of their trip, and the interaction with the Spirit's men before Joe and his family arrived at the bunker. This was the first time in a month that everyone was back home and together.

Earl was pleased to show everyone around the Fort as he called the above ground shipping containers that Dan and he now called home. Earl and Dan had added seven more containers to construct a house from three of the shipping containers and continue the eastern outside wall by two more containers long. The courtyard on the east side of Dan's home was made into a medium sized garden with a small, glass greenhouse in the center. Earl planned to create a series of greenhouses as soon as they could scrounge enough glass patio doors and storm windows. This would extend their growing season by months.

Dan also told them that they had filled the large water tanks with fresh water and added the correct amount of pool shock to keep the water from being contaminated. He also worked on the pumps and diesel generators and had them running. They now had power and running water.

Dan had also traded breeding rabbits and more ammo for solar panels that were placed on the roofs of all of the living quarters. The only thing they were short of was batteries to store the electricity so they could have power at night or a surge of power during the daytime.

"Have you built any windmill powered generators yet?" Joe asked.

Dan replied, "Yes, we have two, but they don't work so well in all of these trees, and they would stand out like a sore thumb in our meadows. I don't want them sticking above the tree line so they won't attract people. We have the two tied into our battery bank to help charge the batteries but don't count on them for any power until we resolve the issues I mentioned.

Joe was impressed. "Earl, I guess you planned all along to set us up for a possible long-term siege. You and Dan have become quite the construction gurus. "

Earl smiled and slapped Joe on the back. "I can't sneak nothing past you. Yeppers, we still have more work to do, but soon we'll have enough water, food, and other supplies to last several months. Ben will hook our indoor toilets and sinks into the existing septic tanks, and we'll be good to go. It don't do no good to get plenty of food and water if you can't get rid of the ... poop."

Joe had a weird look on his face. "You don't think we could use the poop as fertilizer?"

Earl choked and then spit his tobacco juice on the ground. "We have plenty of goat, chicken, and cow shit so no, I'm not playing in people shit."

Everyone broke out laughing except Cobie who had a severe look on her face. "Earl, I thought you'd be the one pushing us not to waste anything including our own waste. Do you really plan to waste our waste?"

Earl stroked his chin as his face turned crimson. "Woman, I know you are pulling my ole leg. But iffen you ain't, you can be the head shit spreader for our crops."

Cobie broke out laughing and punched Earl on the arm. "I guess I'll pass on spreading any more shit until we run out of animal shit."

Cloe jumped into the fray. "Mom you just set a record for saying waste and shit in the same conversation."

Joe beckoned his sassy daughter. "Cloe, I've heard that we've traded many breeding pairs away for other goods. How has that affected our stock?"

"Dad, I'm happy to report that our rabbits are ... err ... breeding like rabbits and we have too many rabbits. Joan and Peggy are making rabbit jerky as fast as they can with Butch's help. We are also set up to can rabbit meat and rabbit stew when the potatoes and carrots are harvested."

"Earl, try to trade rabbits as much as possible and save the ammo. Pretty soon the entire state of Oregon will be sick and tired of rabbit stew, jerky, and fried rabbit," Joe proclaimed

They changed focus, moved to the courtyard on the eastern side of Dan's home, and conducted the rest of their meeting while they lounged in the afternoon sun. It was mid-spring, and the sun felt warm in the cool mountain air. The picnic tables Earl and Dan had built were reasonably comfortable and were set up so they could have large outdoor meals and gatherings. The open area was boxed in by the containers and was about 70 feet long by 40 feet wide.

Joe surveyed the crowd and was pleased that every single one of the two dozen people was a solid contributor to their success. "Let's get started. Before we begin the planning for the Medford situation, I want to know if we've given any thought to all of us moving here into the Fort as Earl calls this place. I love my cabin, but we have many years of fighting and scratching for survival. We stand a much better chance living and working together if we are all here. Then we can slowly recruit friends to move into our cabins. We would use that to get to know them before they are allowed to move up here or know about the bunker. What are your thoughts?"

Ben nodded and spoke up. "Funny that you should ask, we had that discussion while you were gone. All of us feel that there is strength in numbers. We are becoming a very close group and living together as though we are in an apartment building doesn't bother anyone. Earl has the ball rolling with Jed and is a trading master."

Joe liked the idea. "Cobie, let's start bringing a load of our possessions up here every time we visit. We'll make a couple of extra trips today and tomorrow if possible. Great idea."

Dan spoke next. "Joan and I love living up here over the cabin, and Butch likes being close to Peggy. We are becoming just one big happy family."

Cobie elbowed Joe in the ribs and whispered, "When did they move in together?"

Joe shrugged and then smiled. "I'm glad to see that you and Joan are now officially together. Is there a wedding planned?"

Earl broke into the conversation. "I married them while you were gone. We'll have the wedding party tomorrow. I couldn't have them keep living in sin," Earl broadcast much to Joan's chagrin.

Joan's beet red face glowed. "Earl you are a nasty old man. Dan is honorable, and we were just courting. Butch and Peggy are the ones you need to keep an eye on."

Everyone except Butch and Peggy laughed. Their embarrassment didn't last long before they were holding hands and whispering in each other's ears. Cobie's mind was spinning as she remembered that Peggy and Joan were about the same age and were hooked up with the son and father. Cloe stared at Cobie and smiled.

Joe continued the meeting. "I guess we will all be moving up to the Fort as soon as Earl can acquire enough containers for houses and walls. Hell, Earl, you might want to begin double stacking the containers. Wait a minute. Won't the container weight eventually push the railroad ties down into the dirt and make the whole thing cockeyed?"

Earl said, "I'll answer the last question first. Remember we built the Fort on top of the Bunker. I dug the dirt away and laid the cross ties on the concrete that forms the Bunker roof. We don't want to stack them five high, but otherwise, the structure will be solid for a thousand years. If the rest of you move to the Fort, we'll need five homes inside the walls. I think they should all be ground level. We can add sideways to increase the homes and courtyards. Watching Butch and Peggy over there, that could be any day now. Joe, I'm wheeling and dealing with Jed and have a ton of stuff arriving today and tomorrow morning. I didn't trade anything we needed."

Earl shifted his eyes to Cloe and Cole to see Cloe clinging to Cole. He started to add another home to his list but knew Cobie would skin him alive for bringing up the topic. Earl wasn't afraid of anything but Cobie would kill to protect her daughter, and he was not going to tease her about Cole and Cloe.

Earl shrugged his shoulders and changed the topic. "I guess it's time to move on to how we can help the Medford group without getting our asses shot. Joe, you need to lead this part."

Chapter 3

Earl had a two-day start thanks to his guess that everyone would want to move to the Fort once they saw Dan and his homes. He traded over fifty breeding pairs of rabbits, a couple of 1911s, three M3s, and an assortment of ammunition for 36 more containers and enough railroad ties to use for their foundation. He planned to triple the size of the Fort by expanding sideways on the south and north sides instead of lengthways. He bribed Jed with some extra ammunition and an M3 to get a large team down to set up the containers. The men worked from morning to night and completed the project in three days. Earl, Dan, and Ben cut the doorways and windows while Butch, Peggy, Charlie, and Dot hung doors and windows.

Now the whole complex of containers was 200 feet by 240 feet and had six small courtyards and one massive courtyard for gardens, raising animals, or protected yards for kids to play. The containers were in place, but only the homes on the south end were ready to move in at the end of the three days. Earl planned to extend the roof over them before winter.

The three days waiting for the meeting with the Spirit was spent resting, moving furniture, and possessions to the Bunker, and celebrating Joan and Dan's union. Earl filled everyone in on his part of the sniper and tactics training. The second group of sniper trainees told stories about the impossibly long shots they had made and of another attack by the Iranians. This time the attack happened just after they arrived. Bobby took them to a defensive position, and they joined the fight.

The terrorists attacked from three places around the group with only one trying to cross the river, which everyone thought was a diversion until eight old dump trucks with snowblades mounted came charging across the bridge and knocked the barriers out of the way at the middle of the bridge. Bobby and three other snipers using the .50 caliber Barretts with a mixture of armor piercing and explosive bullets stopped the lead truck by riddling the engine and cab of the truck with dozens of well-placed shots. Then they killed the last truck in line and decimated over a hundred men hiding in the dump bed of the vehicles.

As soon as the truck attack was thwarted, the other attackers melted back into the woods and disappeared. Joe's sniper trainees only got a few shots off at the enemy from long range. Zeke's men used a bulldozer to bury the bodies after examining the dead and taking any useful hardware. Zeke was surprised that five of the dead were identified as Iranians. This was the most killed since the first battle at the jet months ago. Zeke was confident that another plane or even multiple planes must have landed.

Dan and Joan's wedding reception was a joy-filled event, and Cobie was pleased that Dot and Joan got along so well. Dot was the same age as Cloe but was more like an average young girl who was too old to play with dolls but too young to date. She was maturing quickly; however, she still acted like a child at times. Cobie had worried about her accepting Joan as a stepmother.

Joan and Dot soon became close friends, and Joan didn't try to replace Ginny as a mother. Joan was a good influence on all three of her new family members. Joan was much more aggressive than Dan on handling criminals and continued her training with Earl to become a better soldier. Dot joined Joan in most of the training sessions, and that helped Dot get over grieving for her dead mother.

Joan had more difficulty with the fact that Butch was dating her closest friend Peggy. Joan knew they were much closer than Dan wanted and was worried that her friend would become pregnant. Joan counseled her friend to be careful and use precaution. Since Butch was now 17 and only a few years younger than Peggy was, even Dan accepted the romance between the love struck pair.

***

Joe couldn't remember having a discussion with his Grandma about her begging him to prepare for an apocalypse, so he was eager to read the next letter.

Dear Joe:

I talked to you today. Your heart was breaking, but you took the time to speak with your Grandma. You didn't say it, but you were still getting over the betrayal from your best friend and that hussy.

You two were never suited for one another. She was a social climber and had enough ambition for five people. Her parents spent most of their money making sure she had the best of everything while they drove beat up cars and barely got by day to day. You, on the other hand, are just a nice sweet guy who is happy as long as you have a place to sleep and food on the table.

Your dad told me numerous stories about how you gave money or your time to help your friends and even some strangers. You are a good man, Joe.

Well, I have to go. I talked Alfred into taking me up to the cabin outside of Prospect. I want to see Marge and her family before I start pushing up daisies. She was very loyal to me, and before me, she worked for your Grandpa. Say hi to her when you go to visit Alfred.

I didn't get a chance to discuss prepping with you. Maybe next time.

Love Grandma

***

Joe directed Earl to set up snipers around the meeting place behind the Motel 6 and Ben to prepare the Fort for an attack in case this was just a ruse to draw fighters away from

36

their community. Joe was a bit paranoid, but it just seemed too easy to save the grandson and then meet with the ghost who leads the resistance in Medford.

Earl had the snipers in place before dawn on the second day and personally scouted the area for threats. He reported that two men were observing the area from across the highway, but one was reading a book, and the other was half asleep. He was confident they didn't see his snipers arrive.

Earl was pleased the potential threat was so disorganized but remembered this group might be joining his group. "Bear, come in Bear."

"Hey Owl, anything to report?"

"Not much. The light is green but there are two sleepy wolves a ways off, and the package arrived a few minutes ago. There are three additional packages."

"I'll be there in five hours," Joe replied.

Joe put the radio back in his pocket and told Wes and Cole to brace themselves for trouble as he pulled out of the trees north of the Medford Dog Park and drove the short distance to the back of the motel. Joe stopped fifty feet from the old Ford Bronco and saw the four men standing behind it.

Joe walked to the men. "I'm Joe Harp, and I'm here to meet with your leader."

The man Cole and Wes had spoken to the other day stepped forward extending his hand. "I'm the leader, and I'm pleased to meet you, Joe. I didn't think that I would be meeting the infamous Joe today. You are a hero among the people of Medford and weakened the gangs so much that we could finish the job."

Joe was surprised. "I am Joe, and I killed my share of gang members and drug pushers. So, you are the one they call the Spirit. What is your real name?"

"You can call me Jeff. Yes, I don't really like the moniker; however, it apparently scares the crap out of the Boss's men so why not make use of it as long as it works. I hear you have a proposition to make to me today."

Joe led Jeff to the pool area behind the hotel so they could sit and talk a while. "Jeff, my group belongs to a larger community that was started by the Mountain Men Survivors Group. Have you heard of them?"

"Yes, even before the Iranians nuked us. Why would I want to join them and what would they expect from us?"

"Tell your guards to hold their weapons out and compare them to ours. Your men have lever action Winchester 30 30s and bolt action 30.06 rifles and an assortment of pistols. We have fully automatic M4s, AR15s, and 9mm semi autos. I'm surprised you haven't captured more weapons from the Boss's men as you killed them. You need modern weapons to fight, and we have them and ammunition," Joe said.

Jeff replied, "I agree the weapons would be a big help. Joe, since we are outnumbered all of the time we make hit and run attacks and can't stay and fight to get the weapons."

Joe was a bit exasperated. "I was alone in Medford and took hundreds of weapons from the gangs. I hit one or two men; I killed them and robbed them. I gave the arms to the locals to fight. With proper training, your team can do the same. Now what we have to offer. We will train your men to fight. We will arm your men to fight. We will fight alongside your men.

Then after you have purged Medford and Ashland of the Boss, we will be trading partners, and you will belong to a MAG. A MAG is a mutual survival group. We will come to your defense, and you will come to our defense. An attack on one is an attack on everyone in the group. We have groups stretching from Keno to Prospect and then down to White City.

I almost forgot. Everyone, including women, is trained to fight above ten-years-old, and everyone above twelve fights or pulls guard duty."

"What will we owe you for the weapons and ammunition?"

Joe laughed. "Nothing for the first batch of weapons, ammunition, medical supplies, and communications gear needed to defeat the Boss. Then you trade for what you get."

"I don't know that everyone in Ashland will agree to the part about everyone fighting or pulling guard duty."

Joe gave Jeff his canned answer. "Then run them off or don't include them in your community. We are not paid police or soldiers. We only fight for the good of the people in our group. If you don't agree with our rules then we will help you defeat the Boss, then walk away from you, and wish you well. We will trade with you but won't come to your defense."

Jeff face betrayed his dislike for what he had heard. "Those rules sound very harsh."

Joe grinned as he nodded. "Yes they are, and if you can't live by them, then your group is not fit to join ours. I damn well won't have my wife and thirteen-year-old daughter fighting to save the lives of worthless assholes that won't fight and die to protect their own."

Jeff replied, "You do know that a few of those damned Ashland socialists survived and won't even touch a gun much less than fight."

Joe firmly answered. "I don't care if they are socialists or donkeys as long as they don't try to harm us. We will ignore them. If you take them into your community and want to join us, they have to obey the rules. If not, kick them out or don't take them into your group. Hell, leave Ashland alone after we decimate the Boss and his men. I don't care. They can smoke their pot and eat veggie burgers as long as they don't cause us problems. If they try to sell drugs to our people or allow gangs to take over Ashland, they will be dealt with harshly. We'll leave now and let your people decide."

Jeff replied, "I'll make the decision for my people after discussing the rules and offer with my council."

Joe was shocked at the answer. "So you're the dictator, and the people have to do what you say? I want to make sure that you know before we would let you join, that our leader and I will talk with all of your people and get their unanimous consent or there is no deal. You need to be thinking about fair elections six months after we defeat the Boss."

Jeff glared, and his jaw jutted out. "How do you have the gall ...?"

Wes cut Jeff short. "I knew you looked familiar. You are that evangelist preacher that was on TV based in Medford. Most of the people think you are a crackpot. Why do you think they will allow you to lead them after the Boss falls?"

"Because my men and I will tell them too."

Joe was visibly pissed and noticed Jeff signaled his men and they started to raise their weapons. Joe scratched his ear

40

and took his cap off. "Jeff, tell your men to stand down. If they make a sudden move or try to attack, our snipers will kill them all. We will help get rid of the Boss and his men, but we won't trade one thug for another. Lay your guns down now and live or we will take your guns and kill most of you in the fight."

Jeff didn't see the snipers that circled the meeting or was smart enough to notice that Joe, Wes, and Cole made sure their own snipers had clear shots at Jeff and his men. Jeff also didn't notice all three of his guests had their 9mm pistols in their chest holsters just inches from their hands.

Jeff's guards suddenly began to raise their rifles and just as sudden blood, bone and brains were splattered all over the area as the snipers unleashed hell on these men. Wes drew first and shot Jeff twice in the chest and once in the head. Cole shot two of the bodyguards, but they were already dead from .308 slugs that ripped their chests open. The snipers hit all of the Spirits men a second after Joe gave the final signal.

Cloe and Joan shot the two snipers belonging to the Spirit. Wes and Cole captured the Spirit's driver. Earl and several of his snipers came down to check on their friends. Joe and the other two cleaned most of the gore off while Earl watched the driver.

The gun battle between Joe's guards and the Spirit's was all one sided. Joe's men fired only because the Spirit's men had drawn their guns. Joe, Cole, and Wes were shooting dead men because a dozen snipers had shot from several hundred yards away with suppressed rifles.

Joe saw the driver trembling with his hands behind his back. "Answer a few questions. Do the people of Medford and Ashland support the Spirit?"

The man gulped. "Yes, they want the Boss and his men gone. They knew they were trading for the lesser of two evils. At least Jeff didn't want the slave trade and drugs to continue. He ruled with his fist but as long as we didn't fight him he took care of us."

"Are there any good men left to lead your community? Joe asked.

The driver quickly answered. "Yes, we have the Police Chief and the Captain who was in charge of the Medford Armory. They are good men and would be a good fit for your group."

Joe didn't trust anyone, but the man appeared to be genuine. "Can you set up a meeting with these men?"

"No, the Spirit has locked them in a room in a warehouse close to where Highway 99 butts against the rail line in North Medford. The building is an older warehouse east of Highway 99 on Sage Road. It's just a block south of where Sage crosses 99."

Wes answered, "I know the building. Will we have to break them out or will they be freed once the Spirit's men hear he is no longer among the living?"

The driver shifted from one foot to the other. "There are maybe a dozen men that were big supporters of Jeff. You just killed half of them. The rest will be in that warehouse."

"Thanks, hey, why did he signal for his men to attack us? We didn't threaten them."

"He told all of us that if your group wasn't going to join us, then we had to destroy your group. He thought if he ambushed and killed you that the rest would fall apart. I think he had plans to take over the entire state once you and the Boss were out of the way," the driver said.

Joe left to talk with his team.

"Damn, we'll have to assault the warehouse and kill those men to have a chance to get those people free," Joe said.

Cole paused to get his thoughts together. "Hey, did any of you watch that movie about where the Israeli Army freed those hostages in Uganda?"

Joe had a smirk on his face. "Cole, we don't have time …"

Earl caught the boy's drift. "Whoa, the boy is on to something. The Israelis made a copy of Idi Amin's limo and had a soldier disguised as the Ugandan president. They drove up with the limo and several vehicles that he usually had traveling with him to contain his security detail. The Israelis drove right up to the terrorists, killed them, and then stormed the building and freed the hostages. Look, we have the Spirit's car, his security detail's vehicles, and his actual driver. We just need someone to play the spirit's role. Wes if you wear his clothes and hat you could pass for him."

"Damn, that might just work. We need five men to act like his guards. We're short on men, so Peggy, you and Joan need to get their hats and tuck your hair. Sorry Cloe, you're too short. Wes will be the Spirit and Joan, Peggy, Cole, Dan, and I will be the guards. Earl, take the snipers and get them in place to back us up. We'll give you an hour's head start.

☆

Chapter 4

Earl's team arrived south of the target and found half a dozen buildings that were perfect for the sniper's positions. Earl spread them out on the rooftops and took up position on top of the warehouse due south of the front door to the warehouse. Earl was only 79 yards from where the two guards were stationed inside the front door.

The driver's job was to pull up to the building and park with the driver's side toward the building about 50 feet away. He was then supposed to wave at the guards and tell them that the spirit was injured and he needed them to help get him into the building. Joe and the other fake guards would get out with most on the side of their vehicle away from the building.

Earl had everyone in place and his silenced AR15 ready to take out the two guards as they rushed to the Spirit's vehicle. The sniper's only had to wait for a few minutes before the vehicles rolled up to the front of the building.

The driver played his part very well. "Bill, Gip, come here quick! The Spirit fell and hurt his leg getting back in the car when the meeting was over. Please help me get him into the building."

Wes motioned for the guards to come to him. The guards were halfway to the car when Earl's rifle barked twice, and the guards fell to the ground. Joe scrambled around the vehicle and shot the men in the head with his suppressed .22 Ruger.

The team followed Joe and Wes as they went through the front door clearing the way. The suppressed rifles weren't silent but weren't heard by anyone, not close by. Joe shot two more guards who tried to fight, and Wes captured another who threw his weapon down. Cole brought the driver in, and the driver gave directions to the several holding rooms.

Cole and Joan killed three more guards, and the fight was over. Joe took the driver to the two remaining guards who threw their guns down and asked the driver to point out any of the Spirit's supporters. The driver pointed one man out. "The rest were forced to help with the dirty work."

Joe shocked everyone but Cole and Earl when he shot the three traitors to their own community. Dan was pissed as usual when he thought there was an injustice. "Joe, why did you kill the driver? He was helping us."

"Dan, think for a minute. The Spirit wouldn't have someone driving him that he didn't trust. He trusted this man who turned against his own people to help the Spirit subjugate them."

"Crap, you're right." was all Dan said.

The warehouse had six large office areas that had been converted to jail cells. Joe and Earl opened the door to the first one while the team covered them. There were twenty men in the room. Joe walked in and looked around. "I'm Joe Harp, and we have captured this prison and killed most of the Spirit's leaders and the man called Spirit. I need to talk with the Medford Police Chief. Please step forward Chief."

A tall, dark-haired man with his right arm in a sling stepped forward. "I'm Chief Ed Brown. What do you want?"

Joe smiled at the man. "I want you to pick three people that you trust to join me in a meeting to discuss your future. I'm Joe Harp, and we want to help you free your city from the Boss and the Spirit."

The man appeared to be confused for a few seconds. "Did you say that the Spirit is dead?"

Joe answered. "Yes, he tried to attack us while we were meeting with him and we had to kill him and his bodyguards. We also killed all of his men here at this warehouse. We need your help, and I think you need ours."

The Chief turned to the crowd behind him. "Ray, I need you and Alex to come with me. Joe, the other person I need is in the women's lockup at the end of the hall. Doris was the Assistant PC and is my right arm."

Joe stopped the Police Chief. "Ed, these people know you, so I want you to stick your head in each room and tell your people that they will be freed after our meeting. Oh, are there any more pockets of the Spirit's men that have to be dealt with?"

"Joe, after my meeting with you, I'll need a short meeting with a larger group of the people that I trust. We need to weed out a few traitors and spies in our group, and then with a bit of your help we will kill the rest of the Spirit's men," Ed replied.

Joe looked the man in the eye and saw a mixture of resolve and relief. "Ed, I'm going to put you in charge of Medford until things stabilize and the town can hold fair elections. Ed, do what you need to now, and you will be able to have your meeting after ours. I plan to make a pitch to you for your city to join our group."

The Police Chief briefly talked with the people locked in each of the cells and joined Joe. "I added a couple of others. I hope that is okay."

Joe looked at the five men and one woman, and they all looked like ex-military. "I assume one of you is Captain Peters from the National Guard."

A man who looked to be in his early forties with short-cropped hair and a scraggly beard stepped forward and said, "I'm Bruce Peters. Captain of Company B stationed at the Medford Armory."

Joe shook the man's hand, which confused the man. "I'm Joe Harp. I'm the man who blew up the armory. I hope you aren't still pissed about that."

"I never was pissed. The gang overran us, and we had to flee and hide. We were glad to see the gang blown to hell but a bit sorry the building had to be sacrificed. What can I do for you?"

Joe asked, "Did any of your men survive that can handle a rifle? We need to take the fight to the Boss."

"I believe there are about a dozen or so locked up here in this damned warehouse. I know the Boss shipped some off to the farms he started around the countryside. Joe, we need to capture those farms as soon as possible so we can feed our people."

Joe waved them into the warehouse breakroom and asked them to be seated. Joe then introduced his team. "This lady is my wife Cobie, Earl is our weapons and training NCO, Cole, Cloe, and Wes are soldiers and snipers. Yes, we all have been in fights with every gang and thug around for fifty miles. Chief, please introduce your team."

"You've met Bruce; he was the Captain of the NG unit. That's Doris; she is the Assistant Police Chief."

Ed finished introducing his people. "Joe, I guess the show is yours."

Joe surveyed the room and wondered if there were any traitors, crooks, or thugs in the group. Before the shit hit the fan, he thought all criminals had a seedy, dirty look about them. In his mind, they all looked like a cross between Al Capone and a greaser biker dude. Joe leaned forward toward Ed. "My group is a part of a larger group called The Mountain Men Survivalist Group. Have you heard of them?"

Several nodded and Ed spoke. "Yes, the State Police watched them for years and found them to be a bunch of harmless doomsday preppers. I always thought they were a bit nutty for thinking the world would come to an end. I guess I'm the nut for not prepping."

Joe replied, "I never gave it a thought myself. My Grandma tried to get me to learn about prepping and even taught me a bit when I was younger. By the time I was an adult I was too complacent. Well, that horse is out of the barn. Now the question is how do we survive and how do we eliminate the criminals, thugs, and dictators who want to rule by fear, murder, and intimidation.

Our people have banded together with the Mountain Men along with several other groups; we are eliminating every thug and criminal we encounter. I know that the Spirit was attacking the Boss's men, but I found out that he just wanted to take the Boss's place. It appears that he locked up about a hundred people here in this warehouse. What was he going to do with you?"

"There was over two hundred men and women arrested when we began to resist the Spirit's tactics and demand for our supplies. I think the women were sold to other gangs and the men murdered or made slaves on the Spirit's farms north of here," Ed reported.

Joe leaned back in his chair and crossed his legs. "I'm going to tell you about the Mountain Men, what we can do for you, and what rules you have to obey to belong."

Joe gave them his standard story about the Mountain Men and then summarized. "I just covered everything. Now these are the points that have to be agreed on. Everyone above the age of 10 has to be trained to fight and pull guard duty. Every group will come to the aid of any group that is attacked. We will give you enough arms, ammunition, and training to defeat the Boss and any leftover Spirit people. We will set up a trading program to benefit everyone. Now a tough one. We don't have prisons or jails. We kill every drug pusher, criminal, murderer, and slaver. If you have a problem with that, then we need to part ways.

If you don't join, we will still help you defeat our mutual enemies, but after that, we will only trade with you. We will not come to your aide if you are attacked. Think it over and if you are interested in going forward, I will talk with everyone after the fighting is done and then go from there."

Ed's people talked for a few minutes among themselves, and Ed stood up. "Joe, these are the leaders of the town, and we want to join you. We will get about 90 percent agreement, and we will deal with the others. Joe, we agree on eliminating the criminals and will kick out anyone who disagrees. You will have a major problem when you give that speech to the people of Ashland."

Joe laughed and turned to his team who were also laughing, "Yes, we figured that from what we know about Ashland. We kind of hoped that the whiny assholes would be in the die off but as it turns out many of the ones that coddle criminals are also hardy preppers."

Joe shook each one of the new team's hands. "Earl, assess their needs. Wes, call Jed tomorrow and get the trucks rolling once you know where a safe place is to ship the supplies. Cole, you and Earl, will stay down here, and be my liaisons with Ed and his team.

***

Joe and Cobie spent the night in a room at the back of the warehouse. They left the others after supper to spend some quality time together. They hadn't been alone for some time, and the walls were thin at Kevin's home. Joe heated some water using his backpack camp stove so they could clean up a bit. Cobie told Joe to wash up first. While Cobie washed, Joe read another of his Grandma's letters.

Dear Joe:

Joe, sorry, but I'm nosey and too old to care so have you found the love of your life yet? Depending on if you are on schedule reading these letters it should be about five months after you received the package with the letters. That's plenty of time to get over a cheating girlfriend and find you a girl. Although if the damned Koreans nuked us, it might slow down the process.

I guess I should write a science fiction novel about the fine art of dating in an apocalypse. Without cars, movies, Chinese restaurants, and such, dating will be like it was back in the 1800's and that will stink. Darn, there won't be any ... uh ... birth control pills after a while and there will probably be a baby boom. That thought made me happy. There could be a little Joe just waiting a few months to be born. I wish I would live long enough to see your children Joe. I know you will be a good father.

I digressed there a bit. When you call tomorrow, I will prod you to start looking for a new woman. You can't live by yourself, that's not good for a man or woman to live alone.

See you in the funnies.

Love Grandma

Joe looked up from his Grandma's letter and saw Cobie standing naked in the soft glow of the candle. He knew his Grandma would approve of his wife and would dote on his new daughter. He gazed at Cobie's voluptuous body and wished her birth control pills hadn't run out.

***

Jed and his team arrived the next day with the supplies and weapons for Ed's team. Ed now had 25 experienced ex-military men and women and twice that many able and willing to fight. Ed's people could only round up a few hunting rifles and some revolvers but not much ammunition; however, Captain Peters men had hidden a cache of six M4s, ten 9mm pistols and plenty of ammunition. Jed could only bring twenty AR15s and sixteen 9 mm pistols.

Earl looked over the weapons and gave the M4s and ARs to the men and women who had military training and then ones with law enforcement training. The rest received the hunting rifles and revolvers. Ammunition was not short, but there was none to waste.

The planning for freeing Medford and the elimination of the Boss started immediately. Joe brought the meeting to order and started the discussion. "Ed, my team will perform sniper duty since we have no military training but are damned good at sniping from a long distance. Bobby and Earl will coordinate Jed's snipers with ours. The Captain will take charge of Jed's and your team. Captain Peters, please take over."

Bruce laid a map of the Medford and Ashland area on the table for all to see. "Bobby will take his snipers into the Ashland area while Earl handles Medford. Earl's mission will be to kill all of the Boss's men they see and to eliminate any targets of opportunity. Doris will lead the guerillas that will infiltrate Medford the night before and kill as many of their leaders at their homes. We will try to avoid collateral damage but will not let potential damage stop the mission. Our Ashland snipers under Bobby's leadership and our Ashland Guerillas under my leadership will have the same mission. We will all kill and disrupt the Boss's men and kill every single one. Do not try to take anyone alive if it puts your life in danger. Any questions?"

There were dozens of questions, and then they split into their combat units to prepare for their individual missions.

The more time Joe spent with Ed, the more he liked the Police Chief. Joe just didn't know if he could trust the man. "Ed, do you have anyone leaking information to the Boss or others in your group?"

Ed leaned forward and stroked his beard. "Remember I said we had to do a little house cleaning at the jail. We just buried nine traitors and informants. Our house is clean. Joe, I have to say that the Boss knew every step the Mountain Men were making. He also knew quite a bit about your people. I think you both have spies."

This pleased Joe that Ed was so forthcoming. "Ed, we found our spy, and she was accidentally killed when we caught her with her contact. Zeke, the leader of the Mountain Men, suspects a spy in his group. I have been tasked with finding that spy. I could use some help."

"My wife has been working as a cook for the Boss. One night she overheard a conversation between the Boss and his henchman, Harry. The conversation led her to believe that someone's son-in-law who is a doctor is the spy. The Boss paid the spy to kill Zeke with poison, but the spy couldn't get Zeke off to himself, so they tried to kill him with a bomb. I don't know how that turned out, but I take it that your leader is still alive."

Joe's eyes widened, and he jumped to his feet. "Sorry, but I have to get a message to Zeke.

Joe caught his wife outside in the shade talking to Cloe and Cole after the first round of planning. "Babe, I need you to go to Zeke and give him a message. Take Cole with you and pick up Dan for the ride. You can take one of the Jeeps and drive along with Jed's team as they head back home. Jed will send an escort back with you to make sure you get home safe. I will give Jed part of the message so he won't question the trip but you must keep what I'm about to tell you to yourself and no one else."

Cobie was intrigued by the cloak and dagger sound of this mission. "Of course I'll keep the info to myself. What is the message?"

"Babe, Zeke's son-in-law, the doctor, is the spy. Tell Zeke we suspect him and for Zeke to leak only to his son-in-law this message and then watch him close. Be careful and then get back home quickly. I'm only giving Earl four of our snipers and ten from our other groups. That leaves over 15 of you to guard our Fort. Gather everyone in the Fort and watch for an attack. The spy will tell the Boss that most of the Mountain Men people will be in Medford supporting this assault on the Boss. This could trigger an attack if we are right about who the spy is."

"Hon, you are playing both ends against the middle."

"Babe, we need to know if we have any other spies. I trust everyone left in our group, but can we trust the others?" Joe replied.

***

Zeke was surprised when Cobie showed up with his returning men and asked for a private meeting. "Cobie what brings you up here sounding so secretive? Amber told me you caught her off to the side and said you urgently needed to meet with me."

Cobie was uneasy telling this man he had a traitor in his group. "Zeke we learned from a reliable source that your mole is the doctor, your son-in-law. Joe asked me to hand this note to you with his plan to verify that the doctor is the spy."

Zeke opened the envelope and read the message. "Tell Joe I read and understand the message. Tell him that I implemented the message a few minutes after you left. If true, this will hurt my daughter but will save our lives. Thanks and thank Joe for me."

Cobie left to go to the trading store and then left with the others an hour later. They arrived safely at the Fort and Cobie called everyone to a meeting. Cobie caught Ben while the others were gathering. "Ben, Joe wants us to hunker down here at the Bunker until the fighting is over in Medford and

Ashland. He is afraid that someone might attack us because they think most of our fighters are in Medford."

"Darn Cobie, this is bad timing. Those three families just moved into Dan and Jane's old cabins. They will be sitting ducks."

"Crap, you are right. We like them, and they are a good fit, but we don't trust them enough to share the Bunker's location with them."

Cobie scratched her ear. "I know! Tell them about the basement at our cabin."

☆

Chapter 5

Harry was relieved that he finally brought some good news to his friend Tom. Since Tom had become "The Boss," he had become arrogant and pretentious. Harry knew Tom back when he was a cheap pimp running a string of skanky whores in Portland. Harry became better at managing his business and money and grew his syndicate into a significant operation. He expanded into Asian sex slavery and supplied women to perverts, movie stars, and brothels across the entire West Coast.

Harry saw the smile on the Boss's face. "Tom, my source snuck out a note that said that mountain group killed the Spirit and all of his leadership. I'd only be guessing what their motivation was and how this affects the rebellion."

The Boss took a pragmatic view of the recent events. "I'll take the good news for now but let's plan for this to go south on us. Those mountain guys have better weapons and organization, so this could get much worse, not better. Get our team together and put a plan together to launch an all-out assault against the mountain group under that Joe character and a larger one against those Mountain Men. Swallow your pride and cut a deal with those Muslims to end this mutual threat against all of our interests."

Harry's veins popped out on his forehead, and he clenched his fists. "Boss, we can't pull troops out of Medford or Ashland. Those damn snipers are cutting us to ribbons. The sons a bitches even have one of those large .50 caliber rifles that shoot exploding bullets. They destroyed five of my two and a half ton trucks and a Humvee just yesterday. We try to find them, and they just attack from behind us. I need a thousand men just to pacify our cities. I'll do what you want, but it will leave us defenseless in the cities."

The Boss saw Harry's bad attitude in his face and body language. "Harry, if we had wiped out their base of operations early on we wouldn't be in this predicament. I want the attacks to begin in two days. No, go get this done."

Harry left the Boss's office, and another man stepped through a door at the back of the office. "Tom, I heard everything. Your man is holding you back. We are a peaceful people and just need a new homeland since your president destroyed ours. After we defeat the enemy, we'll move to Southern California and never see you again."

They shook hands, and the Boss and Islamic Forces were now in league to defeat the Mountain Men. The Boss didn't know that there were only less than thirty of the original Islamic Terrorists left. Their only successes were from forcing men to fight by holding their families hostage.

***

The rest of the Mountain Men snipers and guerrillas were in place the night of Harry and the Boss's meeting. There were over 50 snipers and 100 guerillas that infiltrated the two cities that night. Every group affiliated with the Mountain Men sent some of their best people into the assault. Joe led a five-person sniper team that included Cobie and Cloe. Joe and his loved ones were glad to be ridding the city of the vermin and criminals, but all were sick to their stomach from the constant killing. Joe was pleased that neither Cloe nor Cobie had to do any close up fighting that night. Killing someone in close up fighting was the stuff of nightmares. Sniping was terrible enough without seeing the dead persons face at your feet.

The Boss's men in Medford were all killed before dawn the next day, and the Police Chief spread his people across the city checking for any remaining resistance. Captain Peter's men rolled through Medford at dawn poised to strike the Boss's headquarters.

The snipers and guerillas in Ashland had devastated Harry's command and control. Wes' team had Harry, and several of his men cornered in south Ashland in a restaurant.

Wes radioed Joe. "We have the number two man in Ashland pinned down in a restaurant. Do you want him alive?"

"Not if it places any of you in danger. Make him go away for good," Joe replied.

Wes looked at the wooden structure and then at Cole. "Son, take Joan and make six or seven Molotov's and let's make some crispy critters."

Cole and Joan returned fifteen minutes later, and Wes directed them to light and pitch the firebombs through the windows while the rest of the team kept Harry and his men ducking for cover with suppressing fire. The restaurant went up in flames quickly, and soon the enemy tried to run out the doors to fight or surrender. The restaurant was fully engulfed and lit up the early morning sky as the black smoke drifted east toward the mountains.

"Shoot all of the bastards. No quarter today my friends," Wes yelled.

The snipers in Ashland kept the Boss's men pinned down while the guerillas and Captain Peter's men swept the city clean of the vermin.

Earl leaned against the wall on top of a building about 100 yards from the Boss's headquarters. "Ed, we have the Boss, and about ten of those damned Muslim terrorists pinned down in the Boss's building. I vote that we set some satchel charges and bring the building down on top of the bastards. I'd start the building on fire and a short time later blow the sumbitch to smithereens. Let's don't lose any more men to these cowards."

Ed nodded and patted Earl on the back. "I agree, I'll get my men to bring up some of Joe's homemade bombs, and we'll toss some firebombs in and have a weenie roast."

The bombs arrived a short while later, and Earl grabbed three bombs and led the others to the building under heavy fire. Several of Earl's team were wounded, but only one failed to complete their mission. They threw their glass bottles containing gasoline and a lit fuse through the shattered windows and placed their bombs. Earl was the last one to run from the building.

Earl ran and zigzagged to reduce the chance of being struck by the intense gunfire from the building. He was actually singing the Marine hymn as he approached safety. It was not to be, as Earl was shot in the back several times and fell dead. Earl died as he lived, helping people and protecting his friends.

The fire raged on the lower floors of the building, but the terrorists and Boss's men kept fighting. The first bomb exploded and blew the south wall bricks and glass across the street. The remaining bombs then exploded a few seconds apart, rocked the ground, and assaulted the attacker's eardrums. Smoke and fire rolled from the five-story building as it collapsed down on itself.

Ed had his men retrieve Earl's and a few other bodies killed in the fight and had them taken to the Sacred Heart Catholic Church in Medford for services later. This would be the staging point for all KIA's, and the wounded were taken to the Rogue Regional Medical Center.

The next several hours were spent rooting out any resistance as Ed, and Captain Peter's men ferreted out collaborators and shot them in the streets. Several dozen of the leading citizens of Ashland had assisted the Boss to further their own interests and curry favor with the Boss. They were lined up and executed after a short trial.

Captain Peters had to squash a protest against the executions because a large group of the people didn't agree with the death penalty. They were run off and told to go home or join the traitors and be shot. The Captain had no time or patience for weak-minded people as they closed in on ending the reign of darkness perpetrated by the Boss with the help of many of the city's people.

***

The fighting ended by mid-morning and the silence was eerie after all of the explosions and gunfire all through the night and morning. By noon, Joe gathered his people and took them to the church to pick up Earl's body and take it home with them.

Joe had tears in his eyes as he viewed Earl lying on the table looking so peaceful. "This is a great man who will be missed. I want ..."

Suddenly the radio in Joe's pocket squawked, and they heard, "Joe, come in Joe. We are about to be under attack. We are hunkered down at the Fort, but the Muslim terrorists are all over the damned place. Joe we only have a few fighters they will overrun the place. Please help us. Come quickly."

Joe recognized Ben's voice. "We're on our way now."

Joe didn't have to say much because Cole, Wes, Cobie, and Cloe had grabbed their weapons and were pushing the others to load up and head back home. They were on the road in ten minutes. Ed and the Captain's teams gave them all of the ammo they could spare and a dozen of their experienced fighters were being assembled to follow Joe's convoy up to their homes.

Running the trucks wide open up Dead Indian Road, it only took twenty minutes to reach the quarry when they turned off to head to the cabins. Joe thought the ones at the Fort should be safe, so he wanted to assist the others at the cabins first. They made the turn in front of the quarry and then heard several explosions and then mushroom clouds of black smoke rising then floating east. Joe's heart sank since he knew this had to be a major assault.

Before they traveled another mile, Joe's radio squawked again. "Joe, slow down and roll in carefully. We are mopping up the terrorists and their minions now. Your people are safe."

Joe was confused but recognized Zeke's voice. "We are here to help."

Zeke answered. "No, stay put. You might be hit by friendly fire. We caught the bastards as the attack started and have killed all of the Muslim terrorists. We are rooting out the ones they forced to attack us and dealing with them. Your people are safe. I'll explain in an hour or so. Go on to your Fort and check on the others. Please."

Joe didn't understand everything he heard but felt some relief. "We will comply. Meet us at the Fort when you can."

The trucks rolled up to the container fort and Dan, Ben, and Jane met them.

Joe and his team hugged their friends, and Joe grabbed Ben's hand. "What just happened?"

Ben smiled and shook his friend's hand. "Your trap for Zeke's son-in-law almost worked too well. They caught him trying to sneak the info to the Muslim Terrorists as the Boss had instructed. The only thing that changed is Zeke set them up to attack our community while you were attacking Medford. Zeke called in all available men and women and lay in wait for their attack. They gave us a few minutes warning to get all of our people to the fort and then had us send the message for help.

The bastards were ambushed when they charged out of the forest and attacked the cabins. The doctor didn't know about the Fort, so they concentrated their force on the cabins. That's all I know so far. The fight ended only a few minutes ago, and Jed hasn't called in 15 minutes."

Joe placed his team and the Medford group on guard around the structure in case things changed, but there was no attack. The radio that Jed had given Ben made a squeal, and then they heard, "It's Zeke, we're driving up your road and will be there in a few minutes."

Several Humvees drove up to the Fort and stopped. Zeke, Jed, and Amber climbed out and greeted Joe and the others.

Zeke shook Joe's hand. "We couldn't warn you because the Muslims were monitoring our radios. We gave Ben one of these old kid's walkie-talkies that don't carry over a mile or so and tipped him off as we sent your other people up to the Fort. Those damned Terrorists fell hook, line, and sinker for our trap. We had just enough time to set some explosives and place our troops so we could ambush the sumbitches. We only had one lady wounded, and of course, I executed my son-in-law."

Joe's head was reeling. "Do you really think all of the terrorists are dead?"

"Yes, we attacked their headquarters about five minutes after they charged into your community. Our troops killed every one of the bastards and freed over a hundred women and children. We hated killing the men who were forced to fight, but they shot at us over toward Keno at their headquarters.

The men forced to fight down here dropped their guns. We killed any that kept theirs. Now we have to sort out any sympathizers and collaborators. You don't have to worry about that because we're taking all of the captives back to Keno and figuring it out away from our people. I hope most are innocent, but if not they will be shot."

Joe and his people thanked Zeke and his team before they left. Everyone was dazed, and the relief had not yet set in from their victory.

***

Joe asked several of the Medford men to stand guard for the evening so he could meet with his people. The warfighters took time to clean the grime and burnt gunpowder from their bodies. Joe and his family went to their new home to clean up because Zeke told him that his cabin and Dan's had been destroyed during the fight.

Joe relaxed in the hammock and watched Cloe's rabbits and goats in the courtyard. He quickly decided that perhaps the goats needed to be penned somewhere else after getting a whiff of them. Cloe came out to join him. "Whew, those Billy goats stink. We will need to move the uncastrated males to another place and keep the wethers and does in our courtyard."

Joe looked at Cloe and shrugged. "I have no idea what you said except goats stink."

"Dad, the castrated goats are wethers. The uncastrated males are Billy goats. The females are called nannies or does. They love stinky Billy goats. The stinkier, the better they smell to the females."

"So the worst smelling males get all of the females."

Cloe laughed, "That's about sums it up, but you still have to bathe because female humans don't like stinky men."

Joe replied, "Well, that's more than I ever wanted to know about goats. Let's figure out how to resolve the smell without upsetting all those beautiful nannies out there."

Cobie's nose was attacked by the rancid smell of the goats. "Oh my God, what is that smell? That's horrible. Your turn to bathe. I started some more water on the stove so you can bathe. Damn, I'll need another bath if I stay here."

Joe laughed and said, "It's not me. I stink of manly sweat and stuff. That is goat piss on the Billy goats. I'm going in to take a bath. Please have your daughter find a more suitable place to store the goats."

Joe got caught up on Grandma's letters while resting in the hammock.

Dear Joe:

Joe, back to the Apocalypse. You do know that antibiotics, insulin, and other medications will soon run out and people will begin dying from lack of drugs. The crazy people who take those psychotropic drugs will be climbing the walls. Many will commit suicide, and others will kill people. Pacemakers will stop when the EMP blast occurs or go dead when their batteries die. People will die because they have an infected tooth. Rabies will kill people again.

Most of the deaths will be caused by people robbing, raping, and enslaving others. Hungry people will kill for a can of green beans to feed a starving child. The criminals will take advantage of the chaos to build empires of thugs, slaves, and sex slaves. They will be free to make and sell drugs. The world will go to shit.

Unless you can find a hundred like-minded people to fight these scumbags, the best you can do is to hunker down and hide until the die off is done and then keep away from the large criminal kingdoms that will crop up.

Remember to buy more medicine, guns, ammo, beans, and rice. Perhaps my next letter will be a bit more positive.

Love Grandma

Joe had asked Ed to have Earl's body brought up the mountain, so Sally could spend some time with him before the burial the next day. Everyone in the group visited Earl's home to pay their respect and then gathered in the courtyard between Earl and Dan's homes. They swapped stories about how they'd met Earl and how he affected their lives. The group quickly morphed into an Irish wake with laughter, beer, and whiskey flasks.

Ben and Jane moved over to the table Joe and his family occupied and joined them. Ben leaned close to Joe's ear. "Hey, buddy, don't worry about the Bunker Opsec. We haven't told the new families about the doorway down to the Bunker or the bunker. I'm sure they will be found trustworthy, but I think everyone should earn trust over months if not years."

Joe nodded and fidgeted with his hands. "Ben, I want you to take over leadership of the group. I'm tired, and my give a shit is bruised and begging for relief. I plan to hold a vote next week. I'll nominate you and the vote should go your way."

Ben was dumbfounded. "This is a surprise. I thought you would lead us for years. I'm pleased you have faith in me, but you will always be our leader."

Joe replied, "I'll be glad to assist and help in any way possible, but I don't want the top job. I just want to build my home, tend my garden, hunt, and fish a lot. To tell you the truth the past two days whipped my ass."

Earl's son, Carl, came out and everyone got quiet. Joe walked over to him. "Carl, we're sorry for the noise, but we got carried away with our Earl stories. Tell your mom we'll be quieter now."

Carl shook his head and laughed. "No! This is what dad would want, and my Mom is thrilled that you are holding a wake instead of mourning. My Dad always appreciated the person's life and not their death. Mom and the family will be out in a few minutes to join the group. Could you wait about 30 minutes before you fill everyone in on today's events? I know Mom wants to hear how we fared today. She needs to know that Dad didn't die in vain."

Joe saw hope in Carl's face and nodded. "Carl, your Dad died a hero. I don't have to embellish the story a bit. We'll cover the past two day's events after we give her our condolences."

A bit later Earl's wife and family came out into the courtyard and joined the community. Joe gave a short speech about Earl's selfless sacrifice for his community and provided a personal story about how Earl meant so much to him. "I want everyone to tell a short story about your feelings for Earl."

The stories were heartwarming, and there wasn't a dry eye in the place. Earl made a significant impact on everyone he met. If Earl liked you, he would tease you. If Earl didn't like you, he told you to your face. Earl loved everyone in this group.

Joe gave a brief overview of the events leading up to the last two days and then provided more detail about the fight in the cities. He then passed on what Zeke had told him about the terrorist attack on their community. "Folks, I'm still in a daze because things unfolded so quickly. I'm pleased that almost everything went in our favor, but our community and several others have to honor and bury some good men and women thanks to the thugs who tried to make us all slaves.

We now control everything west of Keno, Medford, Prospect, White City, Phoenix, Talent, and our mountains. Ashland was liberated, but they won't join us because they don't like our rules. I'll make the standard offer but expect them to decline and get mad when we don't provide protection for them.

The Boss and the Muslim Terrorists have been defeated and no longer exist. We will stay on guard and squash any new gangs or dictators that pop up in the future. Now we will keep our weapons close and tend to our families, farms, and ranches. We have to stock away enough food to last through the winter. I want to hold a town meeting in a couple of days. We'll set new expectations and get prepared to hold elections next year to get some structure to our group. For you new people, we plan to add on to the Fort and make new homes for you."

Joe learned later that all of the new people wanted to settle back in their homes in Medford and would be leaving soon. He wished them well but warned them that life in the city would be tough.

The wake went on until the wee hours of the next morning. That event was always remembered as the first day of the new world after the fight for freedom.

The next day was one of rest and recovery from hangovers. Joe still had to meet with the people of Medford and Ashland to ask them to join the Mountain Men. Joe waited another day before making the trek down the mountain to hold the meetings.

The meeting in Medford went as was expected and there were only a few people who didn't want to join. Ed promised to deal with them so there was a calm celebration and then everyone got back to cleaning up the debris from the day the shit hit the fan and months of dictatorship. They also held a vote that day to elect Ed to be their new mayor and Bruce was elected to be their new sheriff.

The meeting in Ashland was a significant surprise. Joe gave his usual speech and received the expected boos from a few in the audience. When he finished one person stepped forward and said, "You and your thugs can leave us alone now. We can run our city our own way and don't need more dictators telling us what to do. The majority of the crowd booed the man, and several fights broke out. Joe and Zeke walked off the stage with their group for protection as several clashes broke out.

Several women walked up to Joe's group. One woman spoke for the others. "Mr. Harp, most of the city wants to join your group. Could you leave for a few days until we come to get you? We need to have a come to Jesus meeting with a minority of our people. This could get ugly, so you need to leave until we can come back united one way or the other."

Joe and Zeke agreed and pulled all of their people out of the city. As they drove away, they heard gunfire.

The small war continued for several days and spilled over into Medford. The ones against joining Zeke's group sought refuge in Medford, but they were turned away. Then a week later, the gunfire stopped, and the next day a truckload of people drove into Medford and asked Ed to set up another meeting with Joe and Zeke. The winners had killed or driven

71

off the people who didn't want to fight to protect themselves or join the Mountain men.

The fight was actually easy because the same people were the ones preaching against gun ownership and individual rights. The funny thing was most of them had pistols and rifles. They were purged, and Ashland joined the group later the next week. The area was now united and secure.

☆

Chapter 6

The next day after the last thug was killed in Ashland, Joe and his team were exhausted and a bit demoralized by Earl's death. They took a couple of days to rest before doing anything. Only the ones pulling guard duty had to work. Since everyone shared guard duty, they all had plenty of time to relax. Even though no one suffered any severe wounds, they all had aching or pulled muscles from the two days of fighting.

Cloe and Cole relaxed in the courtyard and took long walks in the woods. Cloe tended to her rabbits and helped Joan start a Bunny Ranch for Wes' family and Earl's widow. She had moved the smelly goats to the large courtyard, but the rest of the team soon demanded that the goats be placed elsewhere due to their foul smell.

Joe and Cobie rested and took an overdue honeymoon in their new unfinished home. They sent Cloe to live with Ben and Jane for several days to obtain the much-needed privacy. The place still needed a lot of work to finish, but it had a bed, a kitchen, and a bathroom. The honeymooners tried to stay in bed the whole time but had to eat and rest. This was the first time since they fell in love that they had been alone for more than eight hours when they slept.

On the third day, they were fully rested, and Cobie made a honey do list. She handed the list to Joe. "Hon, I want to make this place livable and here is a list of things we need to be done."

Joe gulped as he saw the rather long list. "Hon, is this for this year or the rest of our lives?"

"Smart ass! I'll get Cloe to make Cole help you and maybe we can also get Ben to help."

Joe absentmindedly shook his head. "Babe, everyone is in the same shape. They all are working on their own places. I'll be lucky to get Cole to help."

Four days later the bathroom, kitchen, and two bedrooms were finished. Finished means, the work was done, and they were functional. The walls were covered with plywood or wood paneling. The floors were covered with throw rugs, and the furniture was in all of the rooms except the living room. The toilet flushed, and all of the sinks worked. Wes and Dan ran the plumbing for all of the new homes while the other men helped them with their homes.

The veins in Cobie's neck were raised, and her face was crimson. "Joe, how the hell do we get a picture to hang on a steel wall? I like the safety these containers offer us, but how do you contend with a wall that you can't hang a picture on?"

Joe walked into what would become their living room holding the end of a sheet of plywood while Cole had the other end. "Babe, I thought I told you we were working in the living room. We are adding the plywood on top of a Styrofoam sheet for a bit of insulation, and you can hammer a nail into it to hang a picture. Slow down and work on the other rooms. They are finished."

Cobie laid the hammer and nail down on the table. "Oops, I got ahead of myself. I'll go prepare lunch while you two he-men install the walls. Come on Cloe I need your help in the kitchen."

A week had now passed since the Boss had been defeated. Ashland had joined the group along with Medford. There were no major threats on the horizon. Now everyone could focus on surviving and making their lives better. Building their homes gave them a common purpose and while hard work, it gave them a sense of accomplishment and much needed safety.

The excitement mixed with sheer terror from the attacks and fighting had now been replaced with hard work combined with boredom. The gardens had to be weeded and tended. The animals needed constant care, and fences had to be installed. It was now mid-summer, and some of the vegetables could be harvested.

It was a constant battle to keep the coyotes and wild dogs from attacking the cows and goats. Cloe ran through the perimeter storage container doors into the courtyard by her home and yelled for Cole. "Bring our rifles. Some darn dogs are after my goats."

Cole came running with their AR15s and quickly caught up with Cloe. There was a pack of about a dozen dogs of all sizes tearing a goat to pieces. They were only a few yards from the outer ring of containers and were bold or starving to attack the animals this close to humans. Cole fired a shot into the air, and a couple of the smaller dogs ran away. Cloe aimed and killed two dogs with one shot and kept shooting. Cole joined in, and soon all of the dogs were either dead or run off.

Cloe had a tear flowing down her cheek. "Those poor dogs must be starving to attack so near to us. I hate shooting dogs. I guess the cows and horses have to graze out in the open, but we need a stronger enclosure for our goats, sheep, and pigs. They stink too much to place them in our courtyards. Cole what can we do?"

Cole looked at the wall made from containers. "Babe we need to make a wall as high as those containers around a huge area for the cows. Then we can keep the sheep, goats, and pigs inside the wall at all times and bring the cows in at night."

Cloe beamed with delight. "We could also keep the mamma cows and babies in the corral until they are large enough to fend for themselves. How large should the big corral be?"

Cole found a stick and drew the coral in the dirt. "I would make it about 300 by 400 feet and use containers on one end and fence the other three sides. I would make the inner fence at least 12 feet high and place a six to eight feet high outer fence around it. We could place razor ribbon on top of the inner fence and double stack it on the ground outside of the outer fence. The containers could be used as barns and chicken houses. We want to think big since we will need a lot of animals once we start slaughtering them to eat."

"I hate to think about killing my goats and pigs," Cloe groaned.

Cole's shoulders shook so hard he almost peed himself. "Cloe, I love you so much, but you know we have to eat these animals to survive. You need to stop naming them names like Wooly, Porky, and Bevis and name them Pork Chop, Mutton, and, Roast."

Cole rolled on the ground in laughter as Cloe glared at him. Then she piled on top of him and began tickling him. "I'll teach you to make fun of me."

They tussled on the ground for a few minutes then stopped breathlessly. Cole took her into his arms and kissed her several times, as he said, "Name those animals anything you want as long as I can keep kissing you."

"Cole, let's go over to the pond and skinny dip. You're making me hot, and I need to cool off," Cloe said.

Cole had his face buried in Cloe's chest and hand on her backside when he looked up and saw Jane walking at a fast pace in their direction. "Babe my mom is right behind you."

"Crap, you're making that up."

Jane saw the two drawing something on the ground and decided to join them. Before she closed the distance, they were rolling on the ground and then started kissing. Then she saw her son pawing Cloe and her face flushed, and her nostrils flared. She was so close there was no retreat. "You two look like you are enjoying the summer air."

"Oh crap," Cloe said as she scrambled to get out from under Cole.

"You know in my day we would neck behind the barn or out on lover's lane. You two have no shame," Jane halfheartedly mocked them.

Cloe thinking quickly, as usual, said, "Jane we were working on a design for a coral when you walked up and Cole said something funny. I started tickling him, and the fight was on."

Jane shrugged. "That looked more like a scene from an x rated movie than a comedy. Kids, use some common sense and don't flaunt your love for each other for all to see. Cole is almost a grown man and Cloe you are ...well ... very mature for a thirteen-year-old girl. If I hadn't come up, you two would have been heading into the trees and got yourselves into trouble. I know you don't want a lecture about the birds and the bees, but Cole doesn't need a baby right now, and I don't think you want one now either. I just don't know what to say."

Cloe jumped up, ran back to the Fort, and disappeared through one of the doors. Jane was left there with a very awkward situation with her son. "Cole, I know you would never hurt Cloe ..."

Cole's cherry red face gave away his embarrassment. "Mom, I'm sorry for interrupting. I know you are right and we have to cool it. Cloe is so ... grown looking that I forget her age. Damn, Mom, she's also twice as smart as most of our adults or me. I don't know what to do. I love her and am willing to wait for her to grow older, but she is in a hurry. It's almost like she wants to have sex to keep me from looking at other women. I love her and don't want anyone else. Mom, I need to get away from her for a while to clear my head and to keep what you think might happen from happening."

Jane was doubly embarrassed now since her son had hit the nail on the head with the issue. Cloe was trying to mark her territory the only way she knew how to cling to the man she loved. She held Cole's hand. "Son, I think you are probably right, and that is why you have to be very careful. A year ago, you would go to jail for being intimate with someone Cloe's age. I know the world ended, but we still have values in our little corner of the world, and our people don't realize how young Cloe is when they see you two together. If they knew, Cobie and I would be catching hell."

Cole's face flushed even more, and his heart pounded. "Mom, what do I do? I can't live without her, but I can't have her either."

"Son you need to make her feel good about you only being interested in her and that you aren't ready for sex yet."

Cole gulped and looked down. Jane hugged Cole, laughed, and said, "Lie to her about that part."

"Thanks mom, I will try to avoid those types of situations in the future. Well, not for several years anyway."

***

Cloe went into her home and slumped down beside Joe on the couch. "Dad, can we build a much larger corral with a 12-foot fence. Cole and I just killed a dozen wild dogs for killing two of my goats. Cole designed a fenced in corral, and I think we can find everything we need in Ashland or Medford to build it."

Cloe's face was flushed, and her breathing was heavy. "Hon, did you run all the way back from the field?"

"No, I'm just excited about building the corral."

Joe's eyes rolled back, and his head slumped. "Cloe, are you and Cole having issues?"

"No, but Jane caught us necking and made a big deal about it. Dad, why does everyone think I'm too young for Cole?"

"Baby Girl. Now shut up and listen. Regardless of how smart you are and how mature your body looks, you are still a thirteen-year-old young girl. Cole will legally be a man next year. He could be put in jail for abusing a minor or child rape on his birthday if things get out of hand. Your Mom has treated you as an adult and equal for years. That was wrong. You're still a kid emotionally and need to let your emotional maturity catch up to your brains and body."

Tears welled up in Cloe's eyes, and she ran to her room.

***

Jane went across the courtyard to talk with Joe who was outside cleaning his tools before quitting for the day. "Joe, we need to talk about Cloe and my son. I know I should be talking with Cobie but I know you much better, and I don't know if she will listen to what I have to say."

Joe thought back to his earlier conversation with Cloe. "What have they done now? Did you catch them doing the nasty?"

"Damn you, Joe. It's not funny. I caught them rolling on the ground and Cole was nibbling on her neck with one hand on her ass and the other in her blouse. If we don't stop this now, we'll have a grandkid in nine months."

Joe knew it was time to get serious as he saw Jane's veins in her neck throb and her jaw clenched. "Jane, I'm sorry, but it's not the end of the world if they do decide to ...get together. Jane, we have three choices. One, do nothing, and they will be humping in the bushes behind our back. Two, try to force them apart and they will be humping in the bushes behind our backs because you can't tell two kids to not love each other. Three, my favorite, have our fearless leader send Cole out on missions to grow and protect our community while the lust cools off. I vote for three."

Jane gave Joe a hug and didn't see Cobie walking up behind her. Jane smiled. "Joe you are the greatest leader and father. Number 3 is the way to go. Of course, Cole suggested number three twenty minutes ago."

Jane hugged Joe again just as Cobie stopped behind them. "And who is this shameless hussy hugging my husband. I won him fair and square and will fight for him."

"Cobie, I ... err ... was just thanking Joe."

Cobie had a serious expression on her face then grinned. "Sorry for scaring you. I overheard part of the discussion and saw Cloe run to her room in tears after talking with Joe, so I assumed Joe came up with a brilliant plan to handle the star-crossed lovers. I for one am at my wit's end. I love Cole and want him to marry Cloe in 3-5 years. I'm afraid if we force them apart they will just run away and be at the mercy of the jungle around us."

Jane hugged Cobie as she broke down into tears. "Cobie, we have a plan to subtly keep them apart much of the time until Cloe grows up or the lust cools down."

"Lust?" Cobie asked.

Jane told Cobie what she saw, and Cobie slumped down beside Joe. "So the best solution is to send Jane's son out to join every battle so my daughter can grow up. I want them apart; not Cole shot up."

Jane knew how Cobie felt and said, "Hon, Cole suggested this course of action. I think he knows that they won't be able to control their emotions and wants to get away to clear his head. Joe will also have to promise me that Cole won't go on every dangerous mission. Perhaps he can be a guard on all of the Market and Swap meet days."

Cole was surprised when Jed placed him second in charge of the detail to protect the markets and swap meets in the western half of their community. Cole would report to one of Jed's men, Andy Vine, who had military and civilian police experience.

They had Ashland, Talent, Phoenix, Medford, Central Point and then all the small bergs between White City and Prospect. This meant he had to provide guards for nine weekly meets and one big monthly meet. Ashland and Medford offered several guards for their much larger markets, but Andy and Cole had to provide six guards and a leader for each massive market day.

Each group provided security for the stores that had reopened in their community, but there had been several attacks and robberies, so Zeke decided to assist each market and swap meet by providing trained guards with more firepower. Since the thefts were by low-level drug addicts and meth cooks, it was thought that a show of force would keep them away.

The important thing the service provided to Joe was that Cole had a six-day a week job that kept him away from Cloe and too tired to do anything when they were together.

Andy divided the assignments evenly with Cole, and the show of force appeared to be working. The frequent robberies and attempted robberies stopped a few days after the guards appeared at the markets. Two druggies were shot and killed in Ashland, and after that, it was quiet, and business thrived since families were no longer afraid to bring their children to the markets and swap meets.

***

Cloe worked up the nerve and sat next to Joe on the picnic table. "Dad, could we go to the market in Ashland on Saturday? I want to trade several of my rabbits for some breeding pairs of those New Zealand rabbits. They are very healthy and breed like crazy. We can get six litters a year from those rascals. Pretty please."

Joe saw the devious grin on Cloe's face and quickly understood the ploy. "Well Mom, what do you think? I could use some of that ale that the Ashland Brew Co makes."

83

"Cloe, give me a few minutes with your Dad."

Cloe thought she had pulled a fast one and would get to see Cole at the market. Cobie watched Cloe leave. "Joe she really thinks that she pulled a fast one there. So does she think we're so dumb that we don't know that Cole will be working there?"

"Well, I do want to go and knowing Cole he will be professional and scold her if she tries to get too friendly. Babe, I think Cole has started using his brain to overcome his feelings for our daughter. Cloe is so naive and emotionally immature that I don't think she knows the effect she has on Cole when she flirts with the boy. She is a big tease, and with any other boy they would have,.."

Cobie stood up and pounced on Joe's lap. "Honey, do you know how pissed it makes me when someone talks that way about my baby girl?"

"I ... err."

"Joe, stop stammering and listen. I would be pissed if I didn't see it with my own eyes. The girl works her assets like a grown woman and doesn't realize the consequences. I think it's time to set up a fight between them and let Cloe break up with Cole. Maybe she'll sulk for a while before latching on to another boy her own age."

"Babe, I should have chosen my words a bit more carefully. I must add that you could be jumping from the frying pan into the fire. Another boy may not have the self restraint that Cole has shown."

Cobie kissed Joe. "Hon, I love my daughter, but you don't have to pull punches with me. I know you love her and wouldn't say stuff to hurt her or me. Do I flirt like she does? Did she learn this behavior from me?"

Joe had learned a lot about women in the past several months and answered very carefully. "No dear, I think the characteristic is hardwired into women from birth. You know one of those survival traits. Remember we didn't click at first and then fell in love over time. Sure, I noticed you had a killer hot body and were very intelligent, but we'd both been burned and weren't looking to hook up with anyone. Did I answer the question?"

Cobie saw through the diplomacy and Joe's red face and deliberate speech. "Hon, you gave an excellent and sweet answer."

Cobie laid her head on Joe's shoulder. "Babe, it just dawned on me that no one has been shot at, blown up, or killed in quite a while and we are discussing an ongoing teenaged soap opera. Will the kids go behind the bushes and have to get married, will they break up, will I have a grandbaby when I'm way too young, and finally the one I like best – can my little girl shake her ass as good as her mom? This would be embarrassing if it weren't true."

Joe took a chance to drive a point home. "Babe, several of the older mechanics and office workers back at the shop in Murfreesboro could be overheard most days comparing notes on whose kids had screwed up the most. The list includes two kids in jail for cooking meth, four kids from 12 – 18 hooked on meth, cocaine, and heroine, and one for selling drugs at a high school. Oh, and three of my friends had to raise their grandchildren because their kids were in jail. I think that worrying about two great kids falling in love too early in life pales compared to those poor people's situation with their kids. We have fought and killed thugs, dope dealers, and dictators; surely we can handle two kids with raging hormones."

"I know I should say, "Oh, shit, you are right and suddenly feel better. That's pretty bad that I feel better because my kid isn't hooked on drugs, selling drugs or knocked up by a dope dealer. Joe, you have brightened my day. But Joe we can't shoot our kid's problems or beat them to make them do what we want."

"Hon, take wins where ever you find them. We are the first generation of parents dealing with a nuclear holocaust and trying to raise kids. We are lucky Jane raised Cole so well, or that grandkid would be popping out in a few months."

"I know you are trying to make me feel better, but I don't. I know I raised Cloe very well, perhaps too well. Treating her as an adult and my best friend set her up to believe she is an adult instead of a confused child. I also love Cole more each time you talk. Could we place them in suspended animation until Cloe turns 18?"

"My dear, I aim to please; however, we don't have electricity much less a mad scientist to dip them in a solution and freeze them for five years. Kiss me and forget our troubles for a few minutes."

☆

Chapter 7

Joe was pleasantly surprised when Zeke and Jed dropped in to see him after breakfast on Saturday morning. Joe was taking empty bowls and plates into the kitchen after scraping some eggs and half eaten rabbit into Bennie's dog bowl when Jed drove up in the middle of Zeke's escort. "What do I owe this surprise visit?"

Zeke stepped up and shook Joe's hand. "Joe, I'll get straight to the point. You mentioned that you want to step down from a leadership position. You've let several of your team know your thoughts. Well, your team and mine are worried about who will replace you. Joe, Ben doesn't want the job, and Dan isn't strong enough. Hell, the next strongest leaders behind you and Ben are Jane and Cole, and they aren't ready. For a young man in his mid-twenties, Cole is wise beyond his years. He'll make a great leader in 5-10 years."

Joe laughed and asked, "How old do you think Cloe and Cole are?"

"Damn, Joe I don't have time for twenty questions. My guess is Cloe is around 19 or 20, and Cole is about 25. Why do you ask?"

Joe was not surprised a bit by the answer. "It's about me not wanting to be the leader, please find someone else. I want to just be a follower and not have to make life and death decisions every day. I'll do it until you find someone."

Zeke rubbed his chin as he tried to stay calm. "Joe we need you more than ever to help with this transition to peace time. People are already saying the cost of keeping a standing army is too costly. What can I do to sweeten the kitty to keep you happy while I groom a replacement?"

Joe took his time to come up with his wish list. "I want your permission to requisition all of the overseas containers I can find on the railyards. I only want the containers and will share the contents. I want to borrow the crane and a couple of trucks to haul the containers to our Fort. I also want you to have a crew pickup enough 10-12 feet high chain link fence and hardware to put up a 3,000-foot fence around the Fort."

"Damn, is that all? Do you want us to install the fence?"

Joe laughed as he reached out to shake Zeke's hand to seal the deal. "Yeah, that too.

Zeke laughed and walked to his Humvee. "Joe you could have got a lot more. You sold yourself too cheap."

"Don't worry, I'll think of some more stuff we need," Joe answered.

***

Ben drove the old Suburban down the mountain with Joe in the passenger seat and Jane, Cobie, Cloe, and Charlie in the back. There was an enclosed trailer hitched to the back with the goods they wanted to barter. Jane and Cobie talked about day to day life since the bombs dropped while Charlie and Cloe spoke about rabbit breeding. Charlie was as interested in raising rabbits as Cloe was. He was quite successfully increasing the numbers in his Bunny Ranch. Like Cloe, he sought new breeds to make the effort more efficient.

Cobie couldn't help notice that her daughter acted more like her age around Charlie and they seemed to be having a good time talking in the back seat. She also thought that this on the surface appeared to be a typical trip into town back in the good old days; however, everyone in the vehicle had two pistols and an AR15 nearby.

Ben parked in Cobb's parking lot, and they decided to walk by each vender's table and stopped at each one. The layout of the open-air market was similar to a flea market in the old days. There were 10 by 10 foot squares painted on the pavement and each square held a vendor. Some of the larger vendors rented multiple squares. They saw all kinds of food, kitchen pots and pans, tools, medicine, boxes of stale candy bars, and everything one could possibly imagine for sale.

The sights, sounds, and smells attacked their senses. The smell of bacon frying, BBQ on a hickory fire, and body odor hit Jane in the face like a sledgehammer. Most of the aromas were titillating, but the body odor and dog crap smell assaulted her nose. The dog crap smell came from a vendor selling puppies. He had Shih Tzus and Beagles for sale or trade. Next to him were the rabbit and chicken vendors. Cloe and Charlie peeled off and began dickering for several pairs of the New Zealand Rabbits.

Cobie heard musical instruments, recordings of famous pre-EMP artists singing from solar powered iPhones, CD players, and even a couple of TVs. The sound almost nauseated her since they had only heard crickets, birds, and frogs making noises for over six months. The puppies were barking, kittens mewed, and vendors called out to people to come see their wares. Cobie smiled and began to enjoy the hubbub of the market.

Joe noticed that there wasn't much rhyme or reason to the layout and decided to write a few rules for conducting a market. His input would be that animals and their crap should not be located next to the BBQ stand. He thought for a few minutes then decided he needed to get an improvement team of buyers and vendors to make the rules, but he would insist that animals needed to be located away from the other merchandise. He really wanted a BBQ sandwich until the dog crap odor blew a crossed his nose.

Joe looked across the way and saw Cole giving direction to two of his men who had a belligerent man in tow. As Joe strolled toward Cole, he saw two girls trying to flirt with Cole, and he appeared to like the flirting. He was very disappointed in Cole until he turned to walk away and saw Cloe watching Cole with fire in her eyes. He watched at a safe distance as Cloe drug poor Charlie past were Cole was standing. There was a brief conversation, and then Cloe took Charlie's hand and dragged him away with her.

Joe casually walked past Cole until he heard, "Joe, it's me, Cole. I just saw Cloe and guessed you were here."

Joe hesitated and took a deep breath. "I think it worked."

"What worked Joe?"

"Your plan worked to piss Cloe off by flirting with those two girls in front of her."

Caught, red handed, Cole blushed. "Was I that obvious? Do you think she caught on? I don't want to hurt her, but this isn't going to work."

Joe patted the boy on the back. "I think it worked. I have to guess that you're trying to break it off with Cloe and trying to make it her idea."

Before Cole could answer, several shots rang out, and all hell broke loose. They saw two men run toward a truck parked at the edge of the parking lot. Cole ran past the last vendor, dropped to his knee, and steadied his AR. Both men turned and fired as they jumped into the waiting truck. Bullets whizzed past Joe and Cole striking a large truck, shattering its side window.

Joe was a few steps behind when Cole shot three times, and the truck came to a stop. Cole had shot the driver and the rear driver's side tire. Cole and Joe advanced on the vehicle while several of Cole's guards backed them up. The rest of the guards held their positions in case this was only a distraction for a much more massive attack.

They carefully walked up to the truck and found all but one of the men dead. The driver had a bullet to the head. The man, who jumped into the bed of the truck was ejected and hit a tree head on when the truck careened off the road and struck a boulder. The passenger had several head wounds but could talk.

Cole sifted through the stolen goods. "Joe they were stealing the materials to cook meth. Look at all of the cold medicine."

Joe saw the medicine, and his face grinned all over. "We stopped a significant amount of meth from being made. Damn, the Sudafed will soon run out, and it will take real chemists to make the drug. Cole, you need to get someone to look at your arm. Here let me see how bad it is."

Cole pulled his T-Shirt sleeve up, and there was an angry red furrow about three inches long and four inches below his shoulder. Cole looked down at his shoulder in amazement. "It didn't start hurting until I looked at it."

"It didn't become real until then. You had a large dose of adrenaline surge through your body and were in survival mode," Joe said.

Joe opened his first aid bag, squirted some antibiotic crème on the wound, and place two wide Band-Aids over the wound. "Now you have another scar to impress the ladies."

The two young women flocked back to Cole as Joe keyed his walkie-talkie. "Jed, the market was just attacked in Ashland. Cole killed the men who attacked. They were stealing supplies to make meth. You might want to warn the other markets."

"Thanks, but I just did. We were hit over here in Keno, and I just heard Prospect was hit a few minutes ago," Jed replied.

Joe frowned. "Cole and I are warning the other markets in his group. We caught one alive and are going to interrogate him after we finish calling the others."

"Were you there for a reason?" asked Jed.

"Nope, just doing some routine shopping when they got caught stealing and tried to shoot up the place. Cole quickly dispatched the bastards," Joe replied.

Joe walked back to the passenger side of the truck in time to see Cole sticking the butt of his AR against the man's gashed head. "Talk, and I'll let you go. I don't want you; I want your boss. Tell me who he is and where I can find him and I'll let you go."

The man was scared shitless and babbled on about the hideout. "I know the boss is Jeremy Stackhouse. He stays at the hideout. Let me go, and I'll leave a note telling you where to find him."

Cole pushed the rifle harder against the man's head. The man suddenly screamed and yelled, "Okay! Okay! He lives in Grants Pass, and the hideout is in Gold Hill. I'll draw you a map."

Cole handed him a pencil and paper, and the man sketched out a good map of both locations. Cole took the map and calmly slit the man's throat. Cole forgot that he was surrounded by fifty people watching his every move. The majority of the people cheered, but several women were enraged by what they thought was police brutality. Joe had to take over and calm them down. He told them he and the Mayor would look into the situation.

Joe tapped Cole on the shoulder and pulled him off to the side. "Hey buddy, if you capture a live one in the future, make sure you take him away from the crowd to interrogate and dispose of the bastard. Those women are going to make trouble for us. Remember Ashland has a high percentage of people who didn't support the police before TSHTF and were always looking for police brutality."

Cole's face tightened, and his jaw jutted out. "I guess I could let them take the man home with them so he can be redeemed by their efforts. They could even have him babysit their kids."

"I know you were being sarcastic. Did that make you feel better?"

"Sarcastic, yeah, that's what I meant," Cole replied.

Joe shook his head and then laughed. "Call Jed, Zeke wants to go on the offensive.

***

The ride home was tense at best with Cloe holding back tears and the rest afraid to speak up. Jane and Ben had also seen Cole with the two girls hanging on him. Even though they wanted the pair to cool their relationship they could see her heart was breaking. Charlie tried to lighten up the mood. "Hey, Cloe, I'll bet my Silver Fox rabbits outbreed your New Zealand bunnies. I'll bet a weeks' worth of Bunny Ranch cleanings that mine have more live babies in 90 days than yours do."

Cloe was feeling sorry for herself and didn't speak until Charlie tickled her. "Cloe Bug, did you hear my bet?"

Cloe quickly turned and grabbed Charlie and began tickling both his sides. They were in full grab ass mode having fun. Cloe's mind was off Cole for a few minutes. "Charlie, my bunnies will not only have more offspring, but they will also outweigh yours by four pounds."

"No way!"

"Way!" Cloe shouted and then began tickling Charlie again.

Jane and Cobie had the same "Oh Shit" thought. They both wondered if they had just traded one boy-girl problem for another boy-girl problem. They compared notes later that day.

***

Zeke was on the radio with Joe and was not happy. "Joe, I heard that Cole was flirting with two young girls when the men robbed the market."

This pissed Joe off, his face tightened, and turned red. "Then you heard wrong. Two young girls were trying to flirt with Cole. He tried politely to run them off while still being vigilant. We both saw the men grab the medicine and run. We were fifty feet away from that booth and Cole almost caught up to them when they jumped in a truck that was waiting on them. They fired three shots, one of which struck Cole's shoulder. Cole dropped to his knee and shot three times killing the driver and blowing out a tire. The truck crashed killing another of the men. We interrogated the survivor. He gave us the location of the headquarters and Cole killed the bastard. What do you think should have happened different, Zeke?"

"Yeah, that's the same story that Captain Peters gave me," Zeke said.

This pissed Joe off even more. "Then why were you acting like Cole was derelict in his duty?"

Zeke laughed. "Because those old biddies are putting up a fuss about Cole killing that man in front of them. They took all of the facts and distorted them to suit their need for Cole to be a young rogue cop. I also wanted to see how my Vice President would handle himself when confronted with a tough situation. Now how will we improve on how we handled this situation in the future?"

Joe was speechless, mad, and confused. "Hold the damn phone. What is this VP crap? I'm not going to be a VP. I'm a mechanic."

"Joe, we're going to begin the legwork to form our own country. Hell, man, the USA is dead, and we are the only law in the Northwest. I want you on the team to help me start our own country. We will serve for four years and then hold real regular elections. We'll pattern our country after the original Constitution before all those damned judges started weakening the amendments," Zeke said.

Joe pondered the situation. "Count me in on the planning and doing my part. I'm not qualified to be a government official, but I'll help any way I can. Now back to Cole and the dead thug. Cole handled the situation like we always have. I instructed him that in the future to take the thug out of town and kill him."

Zeke chuckled, "Yes, we'll spread that around. That will work until we can get judges and juries. I don't plan on having any jails. All criminals will either be shot legally or placed on chain gangs or some typed of forced labor to serve their sentences. Any drug, pedophile, rape, and other heinous crimes will be met with death while other crimes will be forced labor."

Joe calmed down and took a deep breath. "Do you need me to head up to Grants Pass to clean house?"

Zeke's voice was calm and deliberate. "No, we need to groom Cole and Jed's boy, Mark, to handle shit like this. Jed will lead a sizable army up there, and Cole and Mark will lead the subunits that hit Grants Pass and Gold Hill. I want us to have future leaders who know how to lead in the field and do the dirty work. I never want fucken' lawyers to run our country. Joe, I want you to concentrate on finishing building Fort Earl and then get ready to be my right hand man."

Joe got a huge smile on his face, "I like that but won't run for office. We'll call it Fort Earl from now on. After all, it was his idea, and he built the first structures."

"Joe, I'm sending a large team with backhoes, bulldozers, and whatever else you need to add on as much as you want to make the place safe and livable. Then you will be free to work on country building," Zeke proclaimed.

"That's a deal. How long do I have to finish construction?" Joe asked.

Zeke answered quickly. "You have six months to finish construction. Of course, you'll have to attend a weekly staff meeting. Jed, Captain Peters, and some of your strongest people should attend. You can bring two with you. Your pick because they will be your team going forward and handle assignments. They will also need to build their own teams. Our first meeting will be to spring all of this on about ten people besides us. I want to get them thinking and then a few meetings down the line we make assignments. We need someone to lead our military, schools, infrastructure, police force, resources, and a bunch of other stuff."

"What will we call this country?" Joe asked.

Zeke promptly said, "Many years ago Southern Oregon and Northern California wanted to break away and form the state of Jefferson. I like Jefferson for our country's name."

☆

Chapter 8

Cole found Cloe back in the corner of their courtyard at her new pen for her New Zealand rabbits. Charlie and Joe helped her build it over the last couple of days, and they built one in Jane's courtyard for Charlie's Silver Fox rabbits. Cole watched the two for a few minutes before walking up to Cloe. "Hey, Cloe I missed you. This darn guarding the markets is eating up our time together."

Cloe turned to Cole with a smile that suddenly changed to a grimace. "Oh, it's you. I guess you finally have time for me. Were those girls too busy to be with you today?"

Charlie sensed the tension. "I'll be back in an hour or so. I need to do some chores for mom."

Cole pulled a chair close to Cloe. "I'm sorry that I have been so busy, but I have a real job to do now. I'm heading up to Grants Pass for several weeks to a month."

Anger and jealousy were etched on Cloe's face. "Will you flirt with girls up there? I thought you only loved me."

Cole gazed at his feet, and he selected his words carefully. "I care for you a lot, but I have a job to do, and Jed counts on me to handle the market security and be a member of our quick reaction forces. Cloe, we have to grow up and be adults fast these days."

Cloe's eyes reddened, and a tear trickled down her cheek. "You wanted me the other day, and we were just about to head to the woods and make love. Suddenly you changed your mind and tried to distance yourself from me. Why? Did your Mom or my Mom get to you?"

"Babe, I care for you and yes I wanted you, but it wasn't right. Cloe, you are thirteen, and I'm 17. Next year I'll be 18 and could go to jail for that kind of stuff. You are too young to be in love."

The tears began to flow. "So, now I'm too young. You didn't think I was too young when your hands were roaming all over me the other day."

Cole cared for Cloe but knew this was wrong. "Cloe that was wrong and we both know it. I think we need to break it off before we do something we will regret."

"So, now we hear the real truth. You are probably screwing one of the older girls. Go, I never want to see you again," Cloe yelled as tears flowed down her ruby red cheeks.

Cole turned to walk away, and Cloe stopped him. "Cole, I love you, and I'll go with what you said. Just boyfriend and girlfriend. Can we at least kiss every now and then?"

Cole's eyes lit up. "Cloe, that works for me. Cloe, I care for you deeply and can see us married years down the road but not now. Do you promise not to try to seduce me again? Frankly, that scared me because I was giving in."

Cloe batted her eyes at Cole as she wiped the tears away. "I promise. I'll be good, and we can just be friends again."

Cole was mad at himself for not going through with the breakup. He knew Cloe had worked him again, but he did care genuinely for her and thought he should give her another chance.

***

"Cole, take Rodney and Butch around to the side of the barn and watch for anyone trying to escape. Keep behind the hedgerow and don't be seen," Jed barked.

Cole saw Butch grimace and Rodney make a face at Butch. "Get your asses up and let's secure our position before the assault."

The tan pole barn was less than a half-mile east of Gold Hill and only a short distance from the Rogue River. The pine straw was thick under their feet but muffled their movement around to the side of the house as they silently progressed through the trees. Cole saw a tree had fallen up ahead and thought it would make great cover and have an adequate view of the barn. "Let's set up behind that fallen pine tree. Keep down, and we'll rotate watching the barn until it's time to get the show on the road."

Butch wasn't happy about being away from Peggy and let his feelings show. "Cole, why do we have to leave our homes and help these people out up here? I could be snuggled up to Peggy in front of a fireplace. Don't you miss Cloe?"

Cole took a deep breath because he needed to watch his comments to Butch. "Sure, I'd like to be with my family but rooting out the thugs and drug pushers makes us all safe. Butch, you are old enough and educated enough that I shouldn't have to explain that every few hours. Stop whining and be ready to fight. I know you have only been married a short time and miss Peggy. Butch, this is what being an adult is all about. Doing the tough stuff when you could be at home with your wife or girlfriend."

"I rather be home doing Peggy than stalking a drug lord. You and Cloe probably don't share a bed, so you have no idea what I'm talking about. Cole, Cloe's just a kid, and you need to find a real woman like I did."

Rodney interrupted Butch. "Butch shut the fuck up. I'm tired of you needling Cole. Grow up for heaven's sake. Hey, someone just peeked out the window. Get ready."

Nothing happened for another hour, then as planned Cole saw the team stage to break the front door down and enter the building. "The shit is about to get real. Check your weapons one more time. There they go."

Mark swung the concrete filled pipe, slamming it into the door just below the doorknob. The door latch shattered and the door swung inward followed closely by eight heavily armed men wearing body armor. There were the sounds of rapid gunfire then silence. Abruptly, the side door swung inward, and three men tried to make a run for the forest. They ran straight toward Cole. Cole tracked the leading man with his AR. "Remember to wound them so we can interrogate them."

Five shots rang out, and the three men fell to the ground writhing in agony from their wounds. Cole kept watching for any more thugs trying to escape before going to check on the fallen men. "Rodney, hang back and cover us while we check on these asshats. Come on Butch. Let's go."

One of the men played opossum and lifted his rifle to shoot Butch when Cole kicked the gun from the man's hand. Cole quickly stripped the men of all weapons and found one had been shot twice in the gut. He didn't have to guess who had killed the man because he heard Butch's rifle bark three times.

Cole was pissed at Butch but kept his temper. "Butch, bury the man you killed while we get Jed over here to interrogate these live ones."

"But ..."

Cole tightened his grasp on his rifle. "No buts. You were supposed to wound him and instead shot to kill. If you think screwing up will let you stay home and cuddle with Peggy you are dead wrong. Get to digging."

Jed saw the two prisoners leaned up against the barn with Cole and Rodney tending to their wounds. "Good job men. Let Bobby and me talk to these thugs. Cole, send those two to the trucks and stay here. I want you to watch the interrogation."

Cole thought he knew how to get information from criminals, but Bobby had the two singing loud and clear and never touched them. "Cole, it's not what you say as much as you convince them you will do what you said you would do."

Cole snickered and then grinned. "Bobby, do ya' think holding your pet rat close to that man's balls had anything to do with him talking so fast?"

Bobby handed his pet rat to Cole. "See Wilber wouldn't hurt anyone, but they didn't know that. I know that Wilber gets pissed when held up by his tail and gnashes his teeth. It's just planting the suggestion that Wilbur hasn't eaten in days that does the trick."

Bobby shot the men in the head with his .22 Ruger MKV and yelled, "Butch, get your sorry butt over here and bury these men when you get done with the other one."

Jed gave Bobby a pat on the back but refused to hold Wilbur. "Get that damned rat away from me. I hate rats. Hey, Cole, are you fed up with Butch yet? I won the bet with Zeke. I bet him that you would handle the lazy bastard and could put up with him as long as it takes. He bet that you would kick his ass in three days. I win a case of homebrew."

Cole nodded and slung his rifle over his shoulder. "I like Butch as a friend, but he is love struck and gets despondent if he's fifty feet from his wife's ass."

Jed replied, "I remember a young boy that was almost as bad last year. You've done what it takes, and I'm proud of you."

Cole cleared his throat. "Jed, the truth is that Earl sat me down and explained life to me and that I had to pull my head out of my rectum. It didn't hurt any that Joe and my Mom have helped by giving me sound advice. I care for Cloe, but I have to shoulder responsibility and support our community.

Now, what did those men tell you?"

Jed whispered, "They told me that the leader was over in Grants Pass at his home with his wife to celebrate his birthday tomorrow evening. We will have to be careful how we handle the snatch and grab. I want the man alive so we can pump him for information on his little empire. We will have several teams hit their three major operations hubs while we capture their leader.

Joe and Kevin will arrive this evening with their crews. Take a breather until Joe gets here and we'll have a brief meeting."

Cole gave Rodney and Butch an update, and then they lay down in the barn to catch up on lost sleep.

Joe brought Wes, Cobie, Joan, Jane, Ben, and Carl with him to add to Cole's two. Joe shook hands with Jed and took his team to the barn to meet with the rest of his team. The three were sleeping fitfully, and Cole rose up when he heard the footsteps. He rushed to hug Jane and Ben and then hugged Joe and Cobie. "Joe, you brought most of the team. I'm glad to see you. This could get hairy if we don't have a large enough force."

Joe patted Cole on the back. "Jed told me that you have done well and extra well putting up with Butch. I'll have a fatherly talk with him and a pat on the back or a kick in the ass depending on how he handles my talk with him."

"Joe, was I ever that bad?"

Joe chuckled. "Hell no! You were love struck but always kept the puppy love out of your duty. Earl's talk with you nipped it in the bud."

"I think I have that behind me now and I'll do my best for you and Zeke."

Joe paused for a minute. "I need a big favor. We are going to try to capture the leader of this group without firing a shot. I need you to team with Joan to fool the man into thinking you two are together and to drive up to his house with a present for him. This will be dangerous for Joan and you but could greatly reduce the bloodshed."

The leader of this group was a very vain man who used his men to take property from others for his own benefit. He lived in a vast home east of Grants Pass overlooking the Rogue River. He had amassed a fortune in gold, silver, and jewels but loved his collection of antique cars the most. The interrogation of several of his men gave Jed and Joe a good picture of the man and his strengths and weaknesses.

Joan drove up the leader's driveway in a 1967 -427 – Nassau Blue Corvette convertible with the white top down. Cole followed in a Wimbledon White with blue stripes 1967 Carol Shelby Mustang GT500 with a 428 CI engine. The rumble of the exhaust was more than the leader could handle. He came walking out of his house followed by two of his guards to see Joan in short shorts and a halter-top leaning against the Corvette. He fell in love with both cars at first sight and had to have them.

"Hey, babe, what are you doing in this beautiful car in my driveway? The car is gorgeous and you ain't half bad yourself. Joan extended her hand and the leader kissed it as Cole walked toward the leader with his palms facing the sky. "Sir, I heard that you are the man to do business within this area. I would like to give you this Corvette as a gesture of goodwill. My boss wants to do business with you and heard that you like fine cars."

"Well, this car and young lady certainly have my attention. That Mustang ain't half bad either. What If I want both of them and the girl?"

Cole stood there in a white linen suit, black shirt, and white tie. "Sir the Mustang and the girl are my personal property, but everything in life is negotiable. We want to see if we can trade fine cars, trucks, and other goods for some of the pharmaceuticals that you are known to produce."

"I want to know more about the group you represent, but I want to drive the Corvette first."

Cole grinned and pointed to the Mustang. "You drive the Corvette, and I'll race you with the Mustang. If I win, you keep the Corvette but meet with my boss. If you win, you get to keep both of the cars, but you still meet with my boss."

"Wait a minute. I'm not a fool. You already know the Mustang will beat the Corvette. I'll take the Mustang, and you race me in the Corvette with the girl in your car."

Cole was pleased with the arrangement. "Okay, there is a street a few blocks south of here where we can race side by side. Hop in the Mustang, and we'll drive over and race. You can have one of your guys be the starter."

"Bill, get in the Corvette with them. Oscar ride with me."

They drove several blocks to where the road was clear of stalled vehicles and stopped side by side. Cole pointed to a gas station sign about three blocks down the road. "The first one to pass that big red sign wins."

"Game on Hotrod. Bill, get out. Oscar, you raise your hand in the air and drop it. We'll take off when you drop your hand."

Cole smiled at the leader. "You might want to buckle your seatbelt this time. We'll be well over 100 MPH when we pass that sign."

"Seat belts are for pussies. Let's get this show on the road."

They revved their engines as Oscar raised his hand. Oscar suddenly dropped his hand, and the race was on. Both cars spun their tires creating a cloud of smoke as they squatted down and launched forward. The engines and tires screamed, and the vehicles went through first and second gears. The cars were just being shifted into fourth gear when the leader saw something that didn't look right up ahead. There was something odd stretched across the road, and it was too late to stop when it dawned on him what the device was.

He tried to brake and noticed the Vette had fallen way behind him as his tires squealed during the hard braking. He hit the spike strip at 60 MPH, and the car blew out all four tires and spun sideways as he wrestled the car to a stop.

Joe looked down at the man. "Keep your hands on the wheel, or I'll shoot your sorry ass."

"What the hell is going on. My men will kill all of you. Where is that crook and broad that swindled me?"

Joe poked the man with his rifle barrel. "You are going to tell us every detail about your operation and everyone you do business with."

"My men will kill you."

There were several explosions and then bursts of gunfire that lasted for several minutes. Joe told the man to shut up until the noise died down. "Those explosions and gunfire were your men dying. Get out of the car and come with me."

Joe walked over to the gas station in time to see Joan come out of the restroom dressed in her regular camo clothes and battle gear. "Joan, don't slap me, but you might want to dress like that for Dan every now and then."

"I already do. The poor thing almost had a heart attack the first time."

Cole came strolling over. "Joe that trick worked to perfection. The man reacted just as you suggested. I didn't have to offer to have Joan ride with me. He wanted to win almost as much as he wanted Joan and the cars. Joan, you need to dress like that for Dan."

Joan giggled and hugged Cole. "Like I haven't heard that before."

The result of the operation was that Grants Pass and the small cities around it were brought into the Mountain Men's control. Joe and Cole stayed in Grants Pass on and off for several months getting everything organized and rooting out the last of the gang and other thugs. Their group of communities was now expanding at a rate faster than anyone had ever anticipated.

☆

Chapter 9

Cloe pounded on Ben's door. "Cole, Ben, please help me! Bennie's in trouble."

Cole came to the door in his underwear with a pistol in his hand. "Cloe, everyone is over at Zeke's today. Didn't Joe and Cobie go with them?"

"Yes, I'm at home alone and scared Bennie will be killed. He chased one of those Cougars away from the livestock and hasn't come back yet. Please help me find him."

Cole quickly dressed and took his AR15 from the gun rack and checked it and his two 9mm pistols before leaving the house. Cloe took him out to the stock pen and showed him the paw prints in the dirt. "This is where Bennie tackled the brute, and they tangled for a few seconds before the cat took off. We need to be careful because the last time this happened, mom got hit by a car and kidnapped."

Cloe took off running with Cole hot after her. Cole caught her by the belt and pulled her back to him. "Babe, stop running. You will have us run in blindly to some kind of danger. Look, I like Bennie too, but we are going to walk fast as we track Bennie and the cat and not be stupid. Let's try to save Bennie without getting one of us killed. I'll go first, and you follow me. I want you to keep a lookout behind and to both sides as we go."

Cloe looked down at her feet. "I know you are right. I'm just afraid for Bennie. I'll follow you and do my part."

The tracks headed northwest on up the mountain into some rough terrain. They had been walking for over an hour when Cole stopped to take a short rest. "Hon, sit down and rest. The cat's lair should be within a mile or two from here. Let's rest for five minutes and then finish our hunt. Cole dropped to the ground, and Cloe stood next to him.

Cole reached up for Cloe's hand and pulled her down. She moved her feet and slumped down in his lap with her arm around him and her head on his shoulder. It was only an hour before the sun went down and Cole didn't want to be this far north of the Fort after dark.

Cloe kissed Cole's neck. Cole pushed her away. "Darling as much as I want to nibble on your neck, we need to hit the road now."

She rose up and grabbed her rifle with Cole rising a few seconds later. "Cloe, we need to be careful. There is no telling what we'll run into up here. There are over a hundred square miles upon this mountain that we haven't explored. We zip down the roads but never get off the beaten path. There could be survivors or dangerous animals up here."

"I'll follow you and be a good girl," Cloe replied.

Cole walked through the thick brush trying to make a path for Cloe, but sometimes the brush would whip back and hit her arms or face. "Oh shit that hurt."

Cole turned to see Cloe on the ground. "Babe are you okay?" Cole rushed to her side and saw the welt on the side of her face. He lifted her into his arms and kissed her injured cheek. "Babe, perhaps we need to rest a few minutes. You are taking a beating from this undergrowth."

Cloe looked at her rugged boyfriend. "Cole, you have a dozen cuts and scrapes, and you aren't stopping. Why should I? Bennie means so much to me."

Cole held her for a minute. "I'm sorry, but I care for you and don't like to see you hurt."

"Then let's get up and get going. My Bennie getting hurt or killed is worth a few scratches."

They traveled a couple of more miles when Cole heard several dogs barking. "Cloe, is one of them Bennie?"

"I don't know. It sounds like several dogs. I wonder if he joined a pack and is still chasing that lion."

Cole took her hand and pulled her forward. "The wind is in our faces so we should be able to get closer to the dogs or lion without them picking up our scent. Come on let's find your dog."

A few minutes later, there was a shot, and the barking stopped. "Someone shot Bennie. They killed my dog the bastards. I'll kill them."

Cole stopped and kept Cloe from blindly running into the person who fired the weapon. "Cloe, they might have shot the lion. You don't know what happened. Calm down and stick with our plan. I'll work us closer to the place the shot came from and maybe we can find Bennie and the person shooting."

A half hour later, they hid behind a fallen tree watching the ramshackle cabin to see who lived there. The tree had been down for years and was covered in slimy moss that felt creepy to Cloe's touch. "Cole, I hate this slimy crap and my butt is soaked from sitting on the ground."

Cole looked in his backpack, pulled out a thermal space blanket, and placed it on the ground by the log. "Here, place your butt on the blanket."

Cloe smiled in the twilight at Cole. "You haven't paid much attention to my butt or the rest of me lately. Are you sure you don't have another woman?"

"Shush Cloe. They could hear us if you speak too loud. I've told you a dozen times that I don't have another woman. I just have my smart assed girlfriend who picks on me all the time."

Cole swatted her on the butt and pointed at the door, which opened. They both saw an old man and woman come outside and walk to the dog pen.

"Marge, I think this new dog will work out real good. He works well with Rufus and Queenie. They treed that cat and held her there until I got a shot off. I'll finish cutting that cat up in the morning, and we'll have 80 pounds of meat and a good hide to trade to those city folks down in Medford."

The old woman replied, "I almost feel sorry for those assholes down there. We been living in the woods for forty years without electricity, cell phones or computers. They fell apart because they couldn't talk on cell phones. That lab was a housedog. Bring him in the house to keep Queenie and me company."

Cole heard the last statement and cursed under his breath. "Damn, I was hoping to steal Bennie back from the pen while they slept. I don't know what to do now. "We'll have to develop a new plan."

Cloe watched the sweet old couple for a minute and laid her rifle down. "Cole, stay here and watch me get my dog back from that sweet old couple."

Cloe abruptly stood up and walked toward the couple. "Hello there. I believe you have my dog. He ran away, and I tracked him here."

The old woman swung around quickly and raised her pistol at Cloe. At the same time, the man took two steps to Cloe and took both her guns. "Well look here Ma. The Lord has brought us a beautiful young woman to help us with the work around here. What's your name?"

Cloe laughed, "I don't need a job; I just want my dog back. If you give Bennie to me, I will be on my way."

Cole watched from cover as Cloe ordered but didn't feel right about the situation and couldn't see much in the dark. Then they moved in front of the light from the open door, and he saw the old woman had a pistol pressed into Cloe's ribs.

Blood raced to his face, and his temples pounded as his adrenaline surged. His heart beat as never before. Then severe frustration set in as it dawned on him that both had guns trained on Cloe. His heart sank as he saw the man lock a logging chain around her neck and lead her into the house. Sure he knew he could have shot both of the scumbags, but Cloe probably would have also been shot.

Cole heard Earl's voice in the back of his head, "*Boy when you don't know what to do, do nothing. Sit down and put a plan together. There are times you rush in shootin' and times to think. This is a time to think.*"

Cole knew he had to get close to the cabin and probe for weaknesses and a way to get Cloe free from these not so sweet old people. In the old man's excitement about Cloe, he had left Bennie in the pen.

The fly in the ointment was the two dogs and Bennie in the pen. He was downwind from them, but they would see or hear him approach when he arrived close to the cabin. He needed a way to silence them without killing Bennie. He had his suppressor for his AR, but suppressed did not mean silent. He could kill one of the dogs, but the others would raise hell, and he indeed wouldn't shoot Bennie unless it was a last resort.

***

The woman had shoved the revolver into Cloe's side. "Raise your hands and don't go for your guns, Cloe. Yes, we know who you are and will sell you to the highest bidder. Now, slowly hand me your guns. The slavers hate the Mountain Men and your father, Joe. Why are you out here alone?"

Cloe handed her two pistols to the old woman as the man kept his gun trained on her stomach. "My dog chased a Cougar, and I got lost trailing him. He's a Lab. Have you seen him?"

The man laughed. "Girl, where you are going you won't need no dog. Hell, you won't need no clothes either. The men who buy nice young girls expect them to be neckid most of the time. Ma, don't bruise her up none. Normally I'd sample a piece of you, but I can see they will pay dearly for a virgin like you. Ma, take her clothes off and chain her to the wall. Place a rag around her neck, so you don't leave any marks from the chain."

Cloe's heart sank because she still had her knife in her boot and had plans to cut the old man's heart out and then slit the woman's throat. The woman ordered her to take her clothes off, so Cloe stalled by taking her jacket off first. Then she unbuttoned her blouse and pulled her shirttail out. She whipped her blouse to the floor and stood there naked from the waist up.

The old man saw her bare breasts. "You're a perky young thing."

Cloe pretended to turn to give him a better view when suddenly she crouched to the floor and drew her knife. She whipped it upward and caught the old lady in the leg. She didn't see the old man's boot flying at her head. Cloe fell to the floor unconscious.

The wound wasn't deep, so the old man bandaged his sister and helped her to bed. Then he came back to the front room to find the other women were tending to the new girl. He untied her boots, pulled them off, and then took her socks and jeans off. He took particular pleasure pulling her panties down and over her feet leaving her naked on the rug.

He looked at Cloe with lust in his eyes but knew he wanted the money more than sex with an unconscious woman. He left Cloe there and took one of the other women to his room.

***

Cole lay on the ground behind the log and covered his upper body and backpack with his poncho so he could take inventory. He hoped looking through his gear might spur a potential solution. He turned his flashlight on and went through his gear between peeking out from under the poncho. His stash of deer jerky, several biscuits, and his medical kit caught his eye. The food could be used to distract the dogs, but they would still bark. Then he saw the Benadryl.

In the back of his mind Earl Spoke, *"Hey dumbass, Benadryl makes people sleepy. Benadryl wrapped in biscuit and jerky, do I have to spell it out for you."*

Cole read the directions, gave up, and placed three pills in each biscuit jerky sandwich. Then he used a couple of small torn duct tape strips to hold the sandwiches together so he could chuck them into the pen. He crept up to the pen keeping a shed between him and the dogs and the wind in his face. Something was going on in the house that held the dogs preoccupied.

The first sandwich landed, and the largest dog took the meal and ran to a corner to chow down. Cole threw the next two quickly so each of the three would get a sandwich, then he slunk back to his log to wait on the Benadryl to work.

Thirty minutes later, all three dogs were fast asleep. Cole threw a rock into the pen, and none of the dogs stirred. He walked past the pen and peered into the window. His hands trembled, and his heart raced as he saw Cloe lying on an old couch along with three other young women.

Cole thought, "What the Hell is this? That looked like an old couple who wouldn't hurt a fly. He walked around the cabin trying to see in several windows. The woman was asleep in a small bedroom, and the old man was sleeping in a more substantial bedroom. Then he saw another young woman chained to the wall. This whole scene was worse than he had ever imagined could happen. He knew he had to free not only Cloe but the others as well.

Cole propped his rifle against the wall and tested the front door. It had a simple string poked through a hole to lift the latch to gain entrance. He pulled the line and entered the cabin. He saw Cloe to his right looking straight at him. She started to rise, and he motioned for her to stay down. He waved and handed her his spare 9 mm pistol and then drew his bayonet and made a throat slitting motion. Cloe nodded.

He pushed open the door and silently walked to the head of the bed. The woman to his right was asleep on the floor. She also had a chain around her neck. Cole covered the man's mouth with his left hand as he drew the knife across the man's throat. The man struggled as blood squirted upward to the beat of his heart. The sticky substance covered Cole's hands. He wiped them on the bedsheets as he saw the man dying.

Cole felt something behind him then heard a noise. He turned to see the old woman with a shotgun. The double barrels looked huge a few feet from his face. He heard two blasts, saw a flash of light, and felt his heart skip two beats as the woman fell to the floor. Cloe stood behind her with the smoking 9mm in her hand. Cole took his jacket off and threw it over Cloe and then found the keys to the locks and unlocked her chains.

While the other women watched, he held Cloe in his arms and comforted her best he could. Cloe was scared but mad as Hell at the same time. Her emotions were all over the place. Her head throbbed and her face flushed with the beat of her heart. "Cole thanks for saving me from these horrible people. They were going to sell me to those slavers. They capture young women and sell them."

Cole looked around the room and saw four naked women staring at Cloe and him. One woman spoke up. "Sir, are you going to sell us?"

Cole was astounded. "Oh, no, we're going to set you free and help you get back to your friends and family. Cloe, get dressed and help me free these women and find some clothes for them."

Cole took the key ring and unlocked the chains on the women. All of them hugged and kissed Cole. Cloe glared, and her jaw tightened. "You've thanked my man enough. Now get your naked asses dressed and behave like civilized women."

Cole was speechless and embarrassed. "Ladies check out the woman's room and find something to wear until we get you to our place. I'm sure we can find you something a bit nicer back home."

Cloe saw the women dressing in front of Cole's eyes. "Cole, please go get Bennie from the pen and turn the other dogs loose. I'm burning this cabin when we leave."

"No, don't burn it. Joe and Ben will want to check it for any information that could lead us to these slavers."

"Okay, but get your butt outside and get my dog."

Cole was a bit dense when it came to women, but he turned to see a pair of bare breasts a few feet away and then Cloe's mad face and finally knew he should get his ass outside if he wanted to live any longer. "Jealous," was all Cole whispered as he walked past Cloe.

Bennie was still unconscious, so Cole borrowed a wheelbarrow to cart the heavy dog home. They were about nine miles from home, and the women couldn't find shoes that fit, so the walk was very slow. To Cloe's displeasure, Cole asked each woman to fill him in on themselves and where they were from. Most were from the Ashland-Medford area, but one was from Tennessee.

Cole heard Tennessee and was all ears. "Where in Tennessee are you from?"

The pretty redhead smiled at Cole. "I'm Kelly Martin and, I'm from a little town southwest of Murfreesboro called Rockvale. I went to MTSU and went to work for a tech company based in Eugene, Oregon. I was hiking when the bombs fell."

Cole was surprised to see someone from Tennessee out in the backwoods of Oregon. "Cloe's dad is from Smyrna and went to school at MTSU.

121

By now, Cloe could see the woman was flirting with Cole. She stepped between them. "Cole thanks for saving me again. I love you so much. Maybe Mom will let us get married when she hears how brave you were today."

Cole cared deeply for Cloe, but this constant drama turned him off. "Why don't you two have a nice discussion and leave me out of it."

The red-haired woman looked at Cloe. "If you need your momma's permission to marry, you're still a baby. A man like that needs a real woman."

Survival of the fittest was playing itself out all over the world, and young women were no exception. The urge to pair up to survive is one of man's oldest hard-wired traits. The red-head was lucky Cloe didn't shoot her to eliminate the competition.

Cole, on the other hand, was sick and tired of Cloe's jealousy and petty behavior. He was also a bit immature and didn't understand the built in survival mechanisms that showed up as jealousy, flirting, and attempting to bond. Cole just wanted calm quiet and peaceful surroundings. He had many years ahead of him before he would get to experience anything like that.

"Hey, there is the road. We'll be at our Fort in a few minutes," Cole said as Bennie stirred and jumped out of the wheelbarrow. "Damn, Bennie, you could have woke up an hour ago."

Bennie jumped all over Cloe as he regained his strength. "Cole thanks for getting Bennie and me back home safe. I'm sorry for being so jealous, but there you were staring at all of those naked women while I was standing there naked also. It made me jealous."

Cole grabbed Cloe by the shoulders. "Cloe, I care for you but looking at you naked made me feel like a pervert. I have to force myself to remember that you are only 14. Don't you get it? I wasn't looking at them as much as I was respecting you by looking away. Grow up and meet me halfway."

"I'm as grown as any of those bitches."

Cloe didn't get it, and that was when Cole knew for sure that he had to carefully back away from their relationship.

***

The community took in the women and made them feel at home while they tended to their needs. Everyone was astounded that the couple could be running a slaver operation so close to the Fort and in the middle of the Mountain Men's home area. Joe reported the situation to Zeke and took a team to their cabin to look for clues. There was a ledger with women, children, and men's names. It also contained a list of the items they received for each of the slaves.

Zeke and Joe sent ten small teams out from every group to survey every home, cabin, and camp for potential slavers. A month later, they were shocked to have found several small groups trading in slaves. The slaves were set free, and the slavers were executed.

Cole took a hot bath that morning and lay down on the couch for a nap. He couldn't sleep so Jane sat down with her son's head in her lap. "That sister and brother kept the slaves in their house and traded them later for food and supplies."

Cole blushed at what he had to tell his mom. "Mom, they were all young women, and they were chained naked to the walls. The man ... err ... Mom, there is no way nice to put this."

Jane interrupted her son. "Sampled the women for his own pleasure before selling them. His sister was in the house all the time this was going on."

Cole's face was cherry red. "Mom, she also sampled the men. They raped everyone except the best looking women and didn't bother them because they brought more money at the market."

Jane's heart ached. "Cole, did they. ?

"No, he didn't want to fight her to have his way. Money outweighed his lust. Mom, these were very sick people. Mom, Cloe got insanely jealous because I saw the naked women."

"But Cole wasn't Cloe naked?"

"Yes, but I couldn't look at her. I wanted to, but it wasn't the right thing to do."

Jane didn't like it, but she understood why Cloe was jealous. "Cole, we've talked. You need to distance yourself from Cloe. I love her like a daughter, but you both need to calm down and grow up a bit before something terrible happens."

☆

Chapter 10

The air smelled much better in the bunker, and the lighting was brighter since Wes had spliced the bunker's electrical panel into the solar power system. Now the lights and exhaust fans worked. He also added a massive bank of batteries to store electricity so they would have excellent lighting when the sun went down. Wes also repaired the toilets, so they flushed adequately and added several more large bladders to store drinking water.

Cobie, Cloe, and Jane were in the bowels of the bunker below the Fort taking inventory of their semi-perishable food supplies while Cole, Ben, and Joe took inventory of all weapons, bullets, and explosives. No one liked the job except when it was very cold or sweltering outside. The bunker stayed at a relatively mild 58 degrees year round.

Ben stopped counting bullets. "Joe, we have most of the containers stacked two high for all housing, but the outside perimeter is only stacked one high. I think we should have some large meeting rooms added to our complex and perhaps several large homes on top. I also think we should make the wall two containers high and place razor ribbon on the walls about ten feet up. Oh, I also want to paint the buildings and walls green camo to match the forest."

That was a lot for Joe to take in at one time. Joe scratched his head and pulled at his mustache. "Damn, I think that is an excellent idea. Earl would like that very much, and it will serve as a monument to our dear friend. Contact Zeke and get the equipment and supplies. He still owes me. How many families could live here when this is completed? Hell, for that matter, how many families live here now?"

We have 16 families now with at least that many homes and apartments empty. The additions would add 10 – 15 more living quarters. I think that would be the maximum we want for the near future. We still want to be picky about who moves in here permanently. We still have quite a few people that have no idea about the bunker's existence."

"I support your plans and agree with keeping the bunker secret. We may never need it, but it makes me feel better knowing we have a fallback position," Joe replied.

Cole listened then leaned toward Joe. "One of the ladies we found at those pervert's cabin told me that her father owned a warehouse up in Grants Pass that was full of industrial solar panels, windmills, and other off the grid products. He planned to open a storefront and sell the products directly from the warehouse but TSHTF before he got it started. She swears the product is still there as of a month or so ago. I'd like to take a team up there to bring it all back here."

Joe nodded but knew he needed to rein in the enthusiasm a bit. "I'm okay with this if you get Ben or Wes to go with you and some armed workers."

"I assumed Ben would go with me. If he can't, I'll get Wes to go."

Ben was eager to get this work done. "Son, I'd be glad to go with you. You know we haven't spent much quality time together since I married your mom. This project will help us get to know each other better."

Cole said, "Dad, I'd like that a lot. Between mom and Cloe they have taken up all of our time when we weren't out shooting thugs."

Joe offered to help. "I'll get several volunteers to go with you, your dad can get the trucks and equipment from Zeke, and you get that girl to go with you to show you where the warehouse is located. Which one is she?"

"She's Kelly, the red-headed girl," Cole mumbled as the women walked up.

Cobie plopped down next to Joe. "Who's Kelly and where are you taking her?"

Joe replied, "You know that red-headed girl that Cloe and Cole saved from the slavers. Her dad has a warehouse full of solar panels and windmills up in Grants Pass. Ben and Cole are taking a crew up there to bring back the entire supply for us to use here and to share with our neighbors."

Cobie tensed up and frowned at Joe. "Joe, we're done counting for the day, and I need a hot bath and one of your special massages."

"Babe, have fingers will massage," Joe replied.

Jane laughed and grinned at Ben. "That sounds good. Ben, you'd better take some lessons from Joe. I need some attention."

Cloe started to speak but knew they would think that she was just a kid and shouldn't discuss adult stuff. She glared at Cole and headed to the bunker's exit. Cole followed her but knew she heard Kelly's name and didn't want the drama, so he hung back and then went home.

Cobie said, "Cloe didn't want to hear anything about Kelly. Do you think it's wise to send Kelly with the team?"

Joe smirked and winked at Cobie, "Come on now. The boy is 17, and he found himself with five naked women. His eyes popped out, and he wished he'd had a camera."

There was complete silence. Three people stared at Joe.

Jane broke the ice. "I'm thinking that Kelly was the one with her tits hanging out in front of Cole. My boy is becoming a good man, but any man would take a peak."

Cobie dropped her hands to her knees. "I can't say that I blame Cloe for being a bit Jealous. If Joe was staring at those huge things, I'd kick her ass and dot his eyes."

Ben leaned back in his chair laughing. "The poor girl was captive and wasn't naked by choice. Poor Cole rushed in to save them all and got an eyeful of those girls and Cloe. Big deal. Nothing happened on purpose. Now don't beat me, but when I was 17, I would have given anything to have been put in Cole's situation."

"Big boy, you are lucky that I'm very secure and not the jealous type or I would kick your ass for thinking about those girls," Jane said.

Joe thought twice before speaking. "I have nothing to say and will not say anything that will stop the bath and massage."

Jane interrupted before Cobie could reply. "Cobie, could you help me teach Ben how to keep his mouth shut at times like these?"

"Maybe we can work out a deal," Cobie replied.

Joe took his walkie-talkie out of his pocket and pretended to key the mic. "Breaker 19. This is Abused Husband; I need to talk to the President. Hey, Zeke, about that shit about adopting the US Constitution. Drop that crappy 19th Amendment and replace it with, "I will obey my husband at all times.""

Ben started laughing, but Cobie glared at Joe while Jane was trying to remember the Amendments. Cobie stood up, grabbed Jane's hand, and walked away. "Those boys will be massaging themselves for a long time until they figure out who really runs this place."

Joe looked over at Ben with a grin and slapped him on the back. "Cobie talks big, but she loves the massages I give. I'll give her until after supper before she forgives me."

Ben frowned and hit Joe on the shoulder. "I wouldn't be so sure about that Skippy. Happy wife happy life, Yes Dear, and keeping your mouth shut would have de-escalated the one up man ship, but no our fearless leader had to throw gas on the fire."

Cobie and Jane kept talking as they walked away. Jane suddenly turned around, stared at Ben, and kept walking as she and Cobie chatted.

"Well fearless leader what's the plan now? Jane and I have never had a fight before, and Sarah was so meek she wouldn't argue with a fly," Ben asked.

Joe laughed and said, "Same here except Cobie is a very tough but sweet person. I plan to ignore her for a couple of days and not perform any manly duties like opening pickle jars and see what happens."

Ben's eyes popped wide open. "My interpretation is that you are going to go kiss her ass, plead for mercy, and rub her feet for a week. You are a chicken shit."

Joe grabbed Ben by the shoulders. "Oh, hell no, that would be an epic fail. You have to apologize for kidding three times and sound as if you mean it. Then kiss her ass, plead for mercy, rub her feet and blame Ben for leading you astray. Then maybe then, she will allow you to be in the same room. Anyway, that's my plan." Joe ran off yelling, "Bye Ben."

Ben took off for his house.

An hour later, Cobie joined Joe on the picnic table and slumped down into his arms and let him rain kisses down on her back and neck. Cobie chuckled as she listened to Joe telling her the story. When he finished, she roared with laughter. "You are a devious, mean little shit. How damned bored are you that you would play such a devious trick on your best friends, Ben and Jane. Buddy Boy, if you hadn't set this up in advance, I'd have been missing my massage, and you would have been sleeping in the hammock for a week. I thought you like Ben and Jane."

Joe tried to glance over his shoulder at the back of Ben's home but couldn't see Ben and Jane. "Are they still arguing?

"No, Ben is pleading for his life from the looks of it. Keep kissing they just looked up. Follow me to the hammock. We need to pile it on."

Cobie turned stood up and led Joe to the hammock where they lay down and started necking until two mad friends showed up. Jane had her hands on her hips. "I smell a rat. How did Joe get back in your good graces so quickly?"

Cobie stroked Joe's chest. "Well, perhaps he made me swear that I wouldn't rat him out when he set that trap about big busted Kelly. Actually, the plan was to drive a wedge between Cole and Cloe, but we should have tipped you off. Then my dumbass husband decided to pile on and pull a joke on you two."

Jane's scowl softened. "So the plan was to screw with Cole and Cloe, not get Ben and me divorced?"

Cobie begged. "Please forgive me. It was all Joe's fault."

Ben and Jane both gave her the finger.

Cobie said, "Then you two bit too hard on the bait so, Joe was then an asshole with his improvising to get Ben in trouble. Then, I had to join in because, well, I'm as bad a person as Joe is when it comes to practical jokes. The damned apocalypse has had us so wound up that fun was low on my list. We're sorry."

Cobie and Jane hugged while Ben stood back then at the last minute stuck his hand out to Joe. "Joe, I forgive you but remember Karma is a bitch. Game on."

With all of the grab ass and fun and games behind them, they settled back down to their original plans to expand the Fort to make it more secure and have the ability to increase their population. Joe made plans for the trip to retrieve the solar panels.

***

Zeke's crew arrived the night before they planned to leave so they would get an early start to Grants Pass. The area was now safe, but they still kept vigilant for surprise attacks. The gangs from Northern Oregon and Washington still probed to find weaknesses, but the Mountain Men responded in each case with overwhelming force. This tactic worked, and the attacks and probes dropped off dramatically over time.

The convoy consisted of three big semis with 53-foot trailers, five large straight trucks, two lowboys with fork trucks and handling equipment, and two Humvees with an eight-man security team. Joe added two Jeeps with eight more people for security. Joe, Ben, Cole, and Kelly rode in one Jeep while Wes, Carl, Charlie, and Joan rode in the other.

Joe rigged the seating so that Cole and Kelly shared the back seat of his Jeep. The ride up Highway 5 was uneventful except for the red face on Cole the whole way up there. Joe asked Kelly about her captivity and maneuvered the conversation to the night Cole rescued them. Kelly gave some great detail about what a gentleman Cole was and how he actually closed his eyes when he turned away from looking at Cloe.

Kelly patted Cole on the thigh and grinned. "He was a pure gentleman. I was standing there naked as a jaybird, and he closed his eyes. He is my hero. Of course, I thought he might have been gay until Cloe set me straight that Cole was her man."

Ben watched Cole squirm. "Jane raised Cole to be a good and very thoughtful man. I have only been in his life for a year, but I am very proud of him and hope that I can contribute to what Jane has already accomplished. Cole, don't blush. You are a good man, and you shouldn't be embarrassed."

Ben made sure the topic was changed, and they chatted about life in general and what Kelly and the other captives hoped to do with their lives. The conversation turned to Kelly's hope to find a husband. Kelly was a lovely and smart young lady. "I know that a man or woman by themselves will be in trouble as the world continues backward in technology. I want to find a good man like Cole to spend the rest of my life with."

Joe was glad that they arrived at the warehouse and Kelly's blatant attempt to tempt Cole had to end. He sent Cole to work with a crew away from Kelly to give the boy a break from her not so subtle ploy.

The warehouse had been raided several times by individuals who needed a few panels and installation supplies, but the small warehouse was still packed to the roof. Ben and Joe raided the front office and showroom to make sure they had all of the product information and installation instructions. Zeke had a decent electrician, but Joe wanted to have a trained repairman and installer in his group. Joan and Carl volunteered to take the training.

Most of the panels were sandwiched between Styrofoam sheets and packed in heavy duty cardboard. They didn't damage or drop any of the panels and quickly filled the trucks. As planned, they left one-fourth of the panels and accessories for the people in Grants Pass to use for themselves. Joe and Zeke agreed to send installation teams back to help after they gained the experience by installing panels at the Fort and Zeke's main base.

They didn't take any of the windmill power generation equipment on this trip but would come back in a week and take half of that equipment. The Mountain Men were scrambling to install enough electricity to begin light manufacturing. It would be another few years before they were able to restart any large-scale production or food processing.

**

The trip back was uneventful and as Joe expected Kelly had told her friends about how sweet Cole was and how she enjoyed the ride with him. Cloe was seething before the trailers were unloaded. Ben, Jane, Joe, and Cobie compared notes and now only had to stand back and watch as Cloe moved further away from Cole. Jane and Cobie's hearts broke for their children but knew this would be the best for Cloe and Cole and might finally end the ongoing Cloe soap opera.

Cloe spent more and more time with Charlie but was so in love with Cole that she kept trying to forget about Kelly and get his attention. Cole treated her as a good friend and not a girlfriend.

☆

Chapter 11

March 2039   One Year after the SHTF

Zeke and Jed finished the discussion over the radio with Joe's counterpart down in Sacramento, California. Zeke didn't like what he had just heard but had to get Joe's group involved. "Joe, come in Joe."

Joe was working under the hood of his old Jeep when he heard the radio squawk. "Hey, Zeke, what do you know today?"

"I know that we'll never teach you how to properly talk on the radio."

Joe laughed. "What else is new?"

Zeke leaned forward in his chair. "Joe, I received some bad news a few minutes ago. Howard down in Yuba City called me to say there had been raids by slavers. The funny thing was they took men and women of all ages and frankly I don't know how to say this."

Joe didn't have time for pussyfooting. "Just spit it out."

"They didn't just take the young and attractive women. According to Howard they only took the strongest people without regard to appearance," Zeke said.

Joe rubbed his beard and scratched his head. "Maybe they've got enough sex slaves and need someone to grow crops. How can you read someone's mind that's so disgusting and ornery? I guess my next question should be – why are you telling me this?"

Zeke gulped then spoke. "I want you and Jed to take a sizeable force down there, find the slavers, and kill the sumbitches."

"Damn, Zeke, that's way down in California. What is that, about 250 miles?"

"Closer to 230 miles, Joe. Howard needs our help and you know he would come up here if we needed him," Zeke replied.

Joe shook his head as Cobie watched. "The timing is bad. You know it's been a year since the grid went down and we are planning to celebrate one year of survival."

"Joe, I'm counting on you. I also have another mission. As you know, we only have a few airplanes in operation and nothing that can carry much. Howard's men have found several old DC3s and C47s at Beale and the McClellan Air

Force Base Museums. Most are part's planes, but his aircraft mechanics have three of them almost ready to fly. The crown jewel is an AC47 Spooky that only needs the new avionics swapped out for the older ones. Most of these planes were stored in steel hangers in pieces that were stored in aluminum packing crates. The electronics on about half were not fried. By God, we're going to have an Air Force and cargo planes."

Joe was impressed. "That all sounds good but what the heck is a Spooky and why should I care about it?"

"Back during the Vietnam War they called the Spooky "Puff the Magic Dragon" because the three 7.62 miniguns shot so fast there was a solid sheet of flame from the plane. The constant shooting also put out so much smoke along with the flames the darn thing looked like a flying dragon. We can only get one of the miniguns working but plan to add handheld missiles and maybe a small canon. We could devastate an enemy without losing a soldier," Zeke replied.

Cobie gave Joe an ugly look, and then Joe spoke. "I'll get the troops together and be ready to travel in two days. Are we flying back?"

"Who would drive that old Jeep back if you fly?"

Joe looked over, saw his daughter Cloe, and smirked. "I can talk Cole into driving it back with some of the troops. He doesn't have anything better to do. Seriously, after we deal with the scumbags, we'll draw straws and half of us will have to drive back. Where are you getting the pilots?"

Zeke replied, "Jed will be waiting for you at the 273 Junction and will have six pilots with him. Remember, about two months ago, we checked to see how many pilots were in the various communities. It appears we have over two dozen fixed wing pilots. Jed will drop them off at Beale before you confront the slavers."

Joe pondered that information. "How many fighters will be joining us?"

"Keno and the headquarters group have 26 volunteers not counting the pilots. They will all meet up at the Highway 273 Junction," Zeke replied.

That pleased Joe and put a grin on his face. "Good, I will have eight counting myself from here, and Prospect, Medford, and Ashland should be able to deliver another 30 or so. Will Jed have a couple of SAWs and plenty of ammunition?"

"And a dozen hand grenades," Zeke stated.

"Cole, wait. I want to give you this to help you remember me."

Cloe handed Cole her last high school picture. "I know the damned school uniform makes me look like a kid, but it's all I have. Please never forget me."

"Cloe, I care for you and could never forget you. I'll keep this picture forever. Good-bye. I'll be back in a week or so."

"Goodbye."

The picture of Cloe dressed in the school uniform skirt, and white blouse drove home to Cole the message that Cloe was only a young girl. Cloe stood there and remembered that Cole said I care for you and not I love you.

Wes pulled his Bronco in behind the Jeep and followed Joe until they turned south on Highway 5 heading south. The Bronco towed a larger trailer with supplies and some trade goods to barter with the California people. Wes' son, Carl, slumped down in the front seat trying to get another hour of sleep while Joan and Butch chatted in the back seat.

Butch was bitching about Peggy not being with him on the trip and how unfair it was on the newlywed couple. Joan closed her eyes and pretended to be asleep. The boy kept nattering about the issue until Joan's veins popped out on her neck. "Butch, shut your mouth and let me sleep. You won't be the first man to go without sex for a week, and you won't be the last. Shut up so the rest of us can enjoy the ride."

"It's not the sex. I just miss her. She is everything to me."

Butch stopped talking for several hours, which suited everyone. The drive was over 200 miles and took eight to ten hours depending on road conditions and any threats encountered. The Mountain Men kept adding small groups from Portland in the north to Sacramento in the south.

It took most of the last year with all of the groups sending teams out to clear cars and trucks from Highway 5. They used farm tractors and a few old wreckers to pull the vehicles off the road. Then each group began clearing the streets in their area. It would take years to clear all of the roads, but it would be worth the work to be able to travel from city to city without having to dodge wrecks and stalled vehicles.

Even though the area had been cleared of all significant threats all the way down to Sacramento, there were still small groups of outlaws that cropped up from time to time and tried to rob travelers. Joe's group always traveled with their full military gear and armed to the teeth.

The large convoy had 12 vehicles of which three were large two to five-ton straight trucks. Half of the vehicles pulled trailers for their gear and supplies. There were 67 men and women from all of the communities under the Mountain Men's control. This force should be able to defeat anything thrown at them with ease.

The convoy stopped south of Redding for lunch at midday. They were making good time and had not had any road issues or threats so far. While the highway was no longer blocked by cars, there were potholes and broken concrete in some areas. The roads topped with asphalt had cracks and frost heaves. This meant that driving very fast was a recipe for a busted tire or a wreck.

The convoy pulled into Yuba City that afternoon and stopped at Howard's headquarters for supper. Howard filled them in on the slaver situation and the airplanes.

Howard was a short, balding Marine Captain who retired the year before the grid went down. "Jed, my man Greg will take the pilots on to Beale to start familiarizing themselves with the planes while we get started on the slavers."

Greg took the pilots with him to the Air Force base, and that only left the group that came down to tackle the slavers. Howard pulled out a huge map and began the discussion.

"Since over 90 percent of the people in the USA have died off during the past year the country is sparsely occupied.

Our only communication is through the shortwave and long-range radios that the Mountain Men gave us. All of the large California cities are smoking ruins containing the dregs of the Earth. We have roadblocks and roving patrols to stop the thugs from coming this way. We have killed a hundred of the criminals and drug addicts trying to come up here and steal. They are poorly armed and have no organization; however, two weeks ago we heard rumors that a new group was kidnapping people from their homes south of Sacramento."

Wes made an ugly face and coughed. "Is this thought to be a new group or some biker gang from San Francisco?"

Howard quickly responded. "We think it is a new group and a well-organized group. We started hearing rumors that a well-armed large group had taken over the area south of Stockton. We even saw a few airplanes fly over our area and head back toward the Stockton airport. A few weeks ago, there were rumors that the group was from the Federal Government and they were setting up a base to help with the reconstruction of Central California.

We sent two small groups down that way to meet with them and determine their intentions. Our men were never heard from again. Then we sent in several two-man recon teams and found that these people were kidnapping the locals and flying them out of here. We've lost a dozen of our group. The funny thing is they take all adults and leave the kids to fend for themselves. They don't take older people or the weak. We think this group needs good strong workers.

The rumors have them based at the Stockton Airport. I would suggest starting there. I can spare 15 fighters from my group and Manny can throw in another 10 from his group in Galt."

Jed looked over at Joe with resolve. "Joe, I suggest that we divide into two teams to search for and destroy this bunch of slavers. I'll lead a team, and you lead the other one. With the men and women from down here, that makes 90 fighters. You take all of your people plus six from Galt, and that gives us each 45 fighters. Both groups will check out Stockton covertly, find the slaver's headquarters, regroup, and attack the sumbitches."

Joe liked the plan but wanted more detail. "Jed, let's take our team leaders and put a more detailed plan together and then brief the rest in two hours. I think we should infiltrate Stockton after dark."

"Agreed," Jed replied.

☆

Chapter 12

Joe's team infiltrated Stockton that night from the northwest while Jed's team came in from the southeast side. Their mission was to seek, find, and destroy the slavers. Both teams would seek friendly locals and question them to see if they knew about the enemy. They took plenty of supplies to bribe the locals and wanted to come back and get them to join the Mountain Men later. The bribes would give some extra motivation for the locals to cooperate.

Joe divided his group into four teams led by Bruce and Doris from Medford, Kevin from the group near Shady Grove, and Wes. Joe kept as many of their own people under their command as possible to facilitate cooperation. Joe only kept Cole with him to have a bodyguard and to help direct the other groups. Joe in effect promoted himself to overall command and coordinated the four group's efforts. Joe wasn't a coward, but Zeke had worked hard to impress Joe with the fact that

Joe was the leader of half of Zeke's group and he needed to direct fighters but not be a fighter unless attacked. This was hard for Joe because he was a hands on type of guy.

The four groups broke down into two to three man teams and spread out through the northwest side of Stockton. The small units reported to their leader and each leader gave updates to Joe via walkie-talkie. The groups fanned out just after dark and began to report to Joe a couple of hours later using runners to avoid their messages from being intercepted.

Most of the reports were updates containing general information about criminals operating in the area, crooked politicians, and food shortages. City people had been late starting gardens and had lost many more people who either died or fled out to the countryside. Wes' group found an area on the west side of town that was rich in rumors and trustworthy information about the slaver group.

Wes sifted through the numerous reports from his team and sent a runner to Joe with a message.

"We have a dozen people telling us there is a major processing center for the slave ring on Rough and Ready Island. It actually is an island but has mainly warehouses covering every inch of the land. There are two vehicle bridges and one Railroad Bridge to the island. We also have five people who swear there isn't any slavery activity going on in Stockton. I think you should head this way ASAP. My runner will give you directions."

Joe grimaced at the thought of people covering up for slavers. "Cole round up Doris' group and have them meet us on the west side of where Highways 5 and 4 meet."

An hour and a half later, Doris' team joined Joe and Wes' team at the designated meeting location. Wes had sent two-three man teams over the railroad bridge to the island to spot any threats.

Wes filled the others in on updated information. "The people operating the slave camp on the island are locals. They appear to be a mixture of motorcycle gangs and corrupt city politicians who banded together after the bombs fell. The citizens killed most of them months ago, but these survived and went underground until the past month.

Several of the locals say that an outside group recruited them to find slaves for work back east. Apparently the die off killed many more people than we thought. This bunch of slavers tell people they work for FEMA and need to relocate people back east to get mines, factories, and power plants back in operation. They seek skilled technicians and strong backs."

Joe sent another four – three-man teams onto the island with instructions to find out where the main body of slaves was kept and to report back quickly. He wanted to seize the place before daylight, and it was already 2:30 am.

Butch, Joan, and Jane came back from the island and reported to Joe. Jane was tired from the constant walking and crouching. She pulled out her map. "Joe, this building houses the guards, and these four buildings hold the slaves. One of the guards gave us this information just before I slit his throat. The guard also said that half of the operation only took volunteers and their families. The other half shanghai men and women to work in factories and coal mines back in Kentucky, Tennessee, and further east. The people leading the effort are ex FEMA and DHS personnel. The body count of slaves and volunteers is low because they shipped over a hundred out yesterday by plane. That's all he knew."

146

Joe met with all of the other scouts and used the information to develop a plan. He sent Cole to take the info to Jed and told Cole to tell Jed that due to timing they had to go ahead and attack without Jed's force to assist. Joe sent Butch with Cole to make sure the message arrived safely.

Joe couldn't give any detail over the radio but did call Jed.

"Billy Boy, this is George," Joe said.

"Hey, George, how's it hanging?"

"Pretty darn good. I'd like to wait on you but this girl is ready now, and I can handle her. Meet you later. I'll send a message with her particulars. Bye Bye."

One of Jed's men looked puzzled. "Man, what the heck did he say?"

Jed laughed. "He said that he was going to attack a group that he could handle and a message was on the way. I assume Cole will arrive shortly with the message."

Joe sent four teams onto the island to take out the roaming guards, the guard quarters, and to free the slaves in the four barracks. The roving guards were taken out quickly with suppressed .22 rifles, and then the guard's quarter was attacked. This also was a non-event since there were only two men awake and five men asleep in the building. They were all dispatched quickly with a .22 bullet to their heads.

Joe had the men's slave quarters freed first by shooting the men and women at their guard posts and then sending a team to infiltrate the warehouse containing the slaves. Joe was surprised that there weren't any guards in the warehouse and had his people wake the slaves.

Joe raised a burning torch in the air and saw most of the men were sleeping, but a few hid behind their bunks. "I'm going to wake the others up. I'm here to free you from these people and set you free."

Joe and several of his people banged on several of the steel bunk beds, and soon every man was awake. Some were frightened, but most were mad and didn't trust anyone. Joe began his talk. "We are from several cities north of here and came to rid the country of the slave traders. Do you want to be free or stay here and be a slave?"

The resounding reply was, "Freedom."

Joe asked, "Do you have families here?"

The answers were a mixed bag of I don't know, maybe, and yes.

Joe said, "We're going to free the others. You need to give thought to what you want to do once you are free. Everyone will be released in a couple of hours. If there are any collaborators in your group, this is your one chance to deal with them now.

Joe left several men to guard the freed slaves and walked into the next building after all of the enemy guards were neutralized. He asked the same questions and received the same mixed answers. Joe wondered how harsh the slavers had been. He asked, "Did any of you lose family members when you resisted the attackers who brought you here?"

Joe was shocked that some of the people didn't resist the slavers. One group of women came forward with one woman speaking for them. "Most of these women and men next door are like sheep and were already waiting for someone to tell them what to do. This group fought the slave traders and killed several before they overpowered us. My husband was killed in the fight, and my son is next door with the men. Most of these people aren't worth your effort. Give us guns, and we'll fight."

Joe was impressed with the lady and left Jane and Joan to check her out and see if she wanted to join his team. Joe then moved to the first warehouse containing families that were supposed to be volunteers seeking a new life through the slavers.

Joe was disgusted as he walked into the building and up to the assembled group of six families. The men of each group walked together to greet Joe. "Sir, why have you attacked our saviors? We have jobs lined up on the East Coast."

Joe had been told these people were volunteers but couldn't believe that they knew the others were slaves. "Wait a minute. I hear that all of you were volunteers, but did you know the same group that you call your saviors also captured people to make slaves out of them?"

The men's leader stepped forward. "Yes, those people didn't have any skills and had to pay for their keep by working in the mines and factories."

Joe scratched his head. "Most of them were going about their lives and didn't need help. These slavers forced them to become slaves."

"But they were needed for the greater good of mankind. After all, someone has to perform the menial labor."

Joe's face burned, and he lost his composure, pulled his pistol, and hit the man across the face with the barrel. "You are worse than the slavers and don't deserve to live. I won't kill you, but I'll let the so-called slaves deal with you and your families."

It took Joe several minutes to calm down before he could confront the next group who also were supposed to be volunteers. He wondered why they had been kept separate from the others. Joe walked up to the group and noticed this group looked vastly different from the others. Their clothes were dirty and a bit ragged, and they seemed beaten down. There were also three times as many people.

Joe gathered his wits and steeled himself for a repeat of the last meeting. "Folks, we are here to free you, but I'm told that you volunteered. What can we do for you?"

A man and a woman came forward. The man asked the woman to lift her arms to Joe. Her arms had several small round burns. She began crying. Joe hugged her and looked at the crowd. "So the bastards tortured you to get you to volunteer. Well, you are now free. We have killed the guards and everyone we can find that worked for the slavers. Do you know where their base of operations is?"

The man spoke, "Their base is in Nashville, Tennessee. Their base here is at the airport, and they have heavy weapons and heavily armed planes and Humvees. Did you kill the traitors next door?"

Joe had a frown on his face. "What traitors?"

The man said, "Those aren't really volunteers next door. They assisted in finding us and capturing us. Most of them were supervisors and managers in the companies where we worked. They knew who had the skills those assholes were looking for. They sold us to the slavers."

Joe knew where this was heading and he liked it. "We will free you first and leave you the keys to their rooms. You do what you want with them. We will check back with you in two days and see if you want to join us. Carl will tell you about our group and where we have groups and cities located."

"Can you leave us a couple of guns? There are some decent people and kids with them, and I promise we won't hurt them."

Joe waved at Carl and Butch, and then all three handed their extra pistols to the leader of the group. "My men will continue guarding the area, but you and the other slaves are free now. We'd like you to join our group where you will be safe and have plenty to eat. As I said, Carl will let you know the good and not so good about us. Stay free."

Cole arrived while Joe was talking with the last group and rested while he ate some jerky. He checked in with his mom and the others filled him in on what they had learned from the captured people. Jane watched her son interact with the others and couldn't help but be proud of him. She walked him away from the others and placed her arm around him.

"Son, are you okay? I am very proud of you. I've been watching you, and I hope that Charlie becomes as good a man and half the leader that you have become. Now that you and Cloe are in the past, you need to find a girl and think about settling down. After all, I will need some grandbabies one day."

"Mom, I'm just enjoying the peace and quiet and lack of drama every day. It's not that I want to be a monk, but I was emotionally drained. There are several women that flirt with me, and I'm not as bashful as I used to be. Mom, don't worry."

Jane's face showed signs of relief as she exhaled and sighed. "Cole, you will be 18 and almost ready to marry soon. You will need a partner in life soon so, please don't give up on a healthy relationship. You will eventually fall in love with the right woman for you.

Cole's face flushed as the blood rushed to the surface to match his embarrassment. "Mom, don't worry. I'll be fine."

Jane patted her son on the back and left when she saw Joe. Jane caught Joe. "Joe, thanks for talking with Cole over the past months. I also talked with him, and I think he has the resolve to move on and find someone his own age. Don't react, but I think he has begun to realize that he needs a mate that can mate and not a child that is smarter than he is. Now stop blushing before you say anything."

Joe was embarrassed a bit, but Jane and Joe were very close friends and could say what was on their minds. "Good for him and we need to support Cloe. This situation could have gone bad if they decided to go out in the woods and, well you know."

"Yes, I know we dodged that bullet. Honestly, I'm surprised that didn't happen. Maybe they'll get back together in four to five years and make us some beautiful grandbabies," Jane wisecracked.

"Shit, we just solved the problem at hand, don't shove them back together."

Cole took a deep breath. "Joe, Jed's crew, has found the operation at the airport and thinks there is only a skeleton crew guarding the place. They should have already attacked and secured the airport and any planes left by the slavers. Jed will come here once he feels the airport is secure and free from further attacks."

☆

Chapter 13

Joe rolled over on the cot and nearly fell to the floor. His underwear and bedsheet were soaked with sweat. Joe had a nightmare that his family was threatened and Cloe was crying uncontrollably. In his dream, he couldn't get her to stop crying, and the enemy was close by and might hear her. Just as they approached, Cole swept in and saved them from a horrible death. Joe lay there for a minute freezing because he'd kicked the sweat-soaked cover off.

Joe's heart was finally slowing down, and his temples stopped throbbing as he tried to make sense of the nightmare. Was something terrible going to happen to Cloe? Was his family in danger right now? Joe had many questions but no answers. He jumped up and went to the jury-rigged bathroom to relieve himself and take a cold shower. The room was warm for March in California but was only in the low sixties. He showered faster than he thought possible and dressed.

Joe walked out to the guard station and spoke to Joan who was on guard. "Hey, Joan, I hope you got a little sleep last night."

"Yes, we only had two-hour shifts last night, and I went to bed a couple of hours early. I did miss my big bed warmer though. Dan may have a fault or two but warming the bed isn't one of them. He keeps me hot all night ...err."

Joe saved her. "I know what you mean I woke up missing my girl. She is always cold but keeps me warm. How is married life treating you?"

"I love Dan and his kids. Butch is like a younger brother, and Dot is my little sister. Dan is so kind and gentle to me. He is the best husband ever. I just hope he doesn't miss Ginny too much. I want to be as good of a wife to him as she was."

Joe thought before he spoke. "Joan, you are a good woman and twice the wife Ginny was. She was too self-centered to be much of a wife to Dan. You have made him very happy, and you can't blast the smile from his face."

"Joe thanks for talking with me. I worry too much and just need to love Dan and his children. Of course, Butch is doing some loving with Peggy now. I'm so happy for them. Now I wonder if I'll have a baby before Peggy. Dan's new child and grandchild will be raised together."

Joe pulled on his scraggly beard. "Jed, 18 of the captured people, want to relocate with us in Medford, and another 9 want to move in with my group. Cole will bring half back with him, and I want to fly the others back with us today. Is that okay with you?"

"Yes, we'll make room on the planes. I'm taking over fifty back with us for Keno and a couple of the smaller eastern groups. I must say that Cole has good taste."

Joe whipped his head around. "Good taste in what?"

Jed hesitated as if he thought he'd said something wrong. "Well, those two Jensen girls have latched on to him and follow him around like puppies. I think he likes the attention. That other girl wears the coveralls and stays to herself. She tries to hide how beautiful she is with the men's clothes. She'll have to work harder to hide that figure, red hair, and gorgeous green eyes."

Joe asked. "How old are those girls? Aren't they sisters?"

"No the ones that dress like women are the sisters. They are Gemma and Jenny. The other one is their cousin, and her name is Molly. She is 19 or 20, and the twins are 18, or so I'm told. Why do you ask?"

"Jed, I think Cole needs to find a girl closer to his own age and those three fit the bill," Joe whispered.

Jed grinned and patted Joe on the back. "Yep, that would make more sense to me, but I'm no expert on young love. Watch them and make sure they are a fit. Their parents were the traitors that were eliminated."

Joe clenched his fists. "Damn, that's too bad, but you think the girls are good people?"

"Yes, the other captives vouched for them. The planes will be ready after lunch. I will add one more, and you can add another hand full of people for the flight back if you want to," Jed said.

"Good, I'll add Jane, Joan, and Wes to the flight back. That leaves me with Cole, Butch, and Carl to shepherd our new recruits back to the community. You still have over 15 of your fighters going with the convoy plus the dozen ex-military from the captives. They will have plenty of firepower to scare off any of the small time thugs that might challenge them."

Joe brought Cole and Jane over to the plane. "Cole, I want you to be the leader of our group that is driving back to Ashland. I'll meet with you and the others to make sure they know who the boss is. All of our people know you and won't be a problem. Some of the freed captives might resent taking orders from someone younger than them, but damn, with that beard, you look much older. Don't tell them your age and give explicit, concise orders and they'll stay in line.

I want you and Butch to take the Jenson girls in my Jeep so none of the single men will bother them. Take good care of them and get everyone home safely. Cole, I love you like you are my own son and I trust you to get this done for me. You are in charge, and you must protect your people. Good luck and stay safe."

"I'll do my best and won't disappoint you, "Cole replied.

Jane looked at her son and was proud of the man she saw standing in front of her. "Son, take care and come back without any holes that the good Lord didn't give you. Try to keep Butch out of trouble, Peggy loves the goofball and is probably knocked up. I love you and good luck."

The airplanes on the runway would have been found only at museums and air shows before the grid went down.

The newest DC3 of the bunch was manufactured in the early 1960's and was now approaching 80-years-old. Of course, they had been remanufactured several times, and every part of the engine had been rebuilt or replaced. The planes looked like the Goony Birds they received their nickname from; however, they were beautiful to Joe and his team. These planes brought back a bit of civilization to them in a world of crap.

Jane kissed her son on the cheek and climbed the steps into the old DC3. The pilot started the engines and a few minutes later taxied across the tarmac to get in line with the other ancient beasts of the sky. Butch and the three women stood there beside Cole as the planes lumbered down the runway and lifted off. The planes circled the airport as they grouped together and then flew out of sight. The sun was barely above the mountains when the last aircraft disappeared.

One of the twins cozied up to Cole. "Cole, please get us to our new home safely."

Cole stammered for a second and saw the disgust on Molly's face. "I'll do my best to get everyone safely to Ashland. If you turn loose of my arm, we can finish loading up and hit the road when Jed gives the order."

Cole then checked on Carl who was loading Wes' Bronco. "Carl, I hope your passengers are better prepared than mine to survive. Those twins have never fired a gun."

"I've got Jack, the leader of the new group, his wife, and three kids. Jack was a grunt in the Army and knows how to handle himself. His wife and oldest boy are armed and can shoot. The bottom line is I'd be scared shitless if Jed, Kevin, and their teams weren't with us. At least you have three hot chicks with you."

Jed had a brief meeting with each of the group leaders. Kevin, Cole, and Bruce listened as Jed spelled out what he expected. "Bruce, your vehicles will bring up the rear with Coles two next. Then Kevin's and then mine will be the lead vehicles. I'll send one of mine out ahead by a couple hundred yards to look for surprises. Keep your fuckin' heads on a swivel and anticipate trouble. This is the time that a bit of paranoia can't hurt. Bruce, you have one SAW, and one of my men will have the other up front. Don't be afraid to use it if needed. Any questions?"

Cole had several. "Jed, do you have an identified threat and will we drive straight through?"

"Great questions. I have a feeling that we didn't get all of those bastards and I'll bet they are pissed at us. We didn't see that gunship that the locals mentioned or any of those Humvees with mounted machine guns. The whole damned operation went too smoothly to suit me. None of those guards was experienced or military vets.

Cole, I think you are right. We will drive straight through and only stop a couple of times to take piss stops. Grab a bucket from the mess area and tell everyone they can hold it or use the bucket. Eat and drink on the move and change drivers when we stop. If a vehicle stalls or dies, quickly transfer the passengers and cargo to the closest two vehicles. Bruce, don't let anyone hold up the tail end of the convoy."

"Will do, sir," Bruce replied.

Jed looked over his group. "Let's hit the dusty trail. We're burning daylight."

Cole walked back down the column to his Jeep and saw that Butch was in the back seat with the twins and Molly was in the passenger seat. She had an old Army jacket and boonie cap pulled down to her ears. She didn't speak as he walked up.

Cole said, "This is the last chance to take a leak before we hit the road. We're only stopping a couple of times for bathroom breaks, and you have to eat on the road. Butch you and I'll trade up driving every time we stop. Girls, Jed gave us a bucket in case you can't make it to the next pee break. Let's roll."

No one had to relieve themselves, and the convoy rolled out five minutes later. Jed led the column up Highway 99 instead of cutting over to Highway 5, and Yuba City was soon out of sight. Jed knew that Howard's men had cleared the Highway all the way to Red Bluff where they would get back on Highway 5. They traveled about 42 miles without any problems and only saw the occasional farmer tending his land.

Things changed when they entered Chico. Cole suddenly got a feeling they were being watched. A half mile into the city Molly grabbed his arm. "Cole, there is a vehicle following us one street over. I think it's one of those Humvees. Damn, there was a man in a window back there with a gun ..."

Molly was cut short by several explosions and rapid gunfire. The Jeep suddenly veered right and struck an abandoned car. Before Butch or Cole could raise their guns, several armed men were all around them. Molly screamed at her cousins. "Run girls!"

Molly drew her pistol, shot at one of the men, and missed. Cole pulled his gun and surged at the man who raised his pistol to shoot Molly. The man fired just as Cole tackled him. The bullet grazed Cole's head, and he fell to the ground.

Another man grabbed Molly from behind and stripped her pistol from her. The twins only ran a few yards before they were captured.

The leader of the group walked over to the men. "Every one of these men is worth a small fortune to us. The women are worth much more. If you kill one, I'll kill you, asshole. Now check them for weapons and see if that one is still alive"

Cole slowly lowered his right hand to reach his chest rig pistol when a rifle butt struck him on the back of the head.

"This son of a bitch tried to reach for a gun. Now he has two boo-boos on his noggin. Load 'em up and take them to the barn. This is a big haul, and we'll have a party once we get their asses on the plane.

Jed and his team had to flee because they were outgunned and outnumbered.

****

Zeke's planes landed at the Medford Jackson County airport an hour and a half later. Joe enjoyed the view as the aircraft flew at 5,000 feet. He tried the walkie-talkie several times without luck. He guessed the storm they flew through north of Redding was the reason for the poor reception.

Everyone left the planes and walked to a line of trucks that came to meet them. Joe saw Cobie sitting in Wes' pickup and waved at her. "Babe, I missed you."

Joe hugged and kissed his wife before pitching his gear in the trailer hitched to Wes' truck. Wes drove with Cobie sandwiched between them. Cloe rode in the back of the truck with the rest of their crew on the way back home. The drive to the Fort was a little less than an hour and was uneventful. Joe filled Cobie in on their accomplishments. "Babe, what would you think about taking in some orphan girls?"

"You know I want to help if we can. You said, girls. How many and how old are they?"

Joe stroked his beard. "I'm guessing the twins are somewhere around 17 and their older cousin is about 19. They appear to be good kids, and they need a place to stay until we can figure out how to deal with orphans."

Cobie thought for a few seconds then whispered. "The girls are welcome and might be of some interest to Cole."

Joe looked over at Wes then whispered in Cobie's ear. "They are riding back here in Cole's Jeep. I don't know what happened to her parents or the twins mom and dad, but they were about to be sold to some perverts for you know what."

"Babe, they are welcome as long as they behave and contribute around the house and gardens. Perhaps the older one needs to stay at Ben and Jane's home so Cole won't be over at our house."

"Oh, shit. Good catch. It also puts them together. I think Cole will like this red-head."

They parked the truck inside the wall of storage containers that circled the Fort and began unloading their gear from the trailer. Cobie and Cloe prepared lunch while Joe put his gear away and cleaned his guns. He was seated at the picnic table when Wes came walking across the courtyard with a concerned look on his face.

Wes gulped and placed a hand on Joe's shoulder. "Joe, our convoy was ambushed near Chico. Jed reports that several Humvees with turret mounted SAWs and one with a Ma Duce shot the hell out of the back end of the convoy. They were also attacked from several positions along the full length of the column. The column escaped, but several of the trailing vehicles didn't make it."

Joe was shocked, and his eyes popped wide open. "What about Cole and the rest of my team?"

"Joe, we just don't know yet. Both of your vehicles were lost to the attacking force, but we don't know if anyone survived or might have been taken captive."

Jane and Ben ran into the courtyard from across the way and ran up to Wes. "Have you heard anything from Cole, yet? Is he okay?"

"Jane, I'm sorry, but Cole is among the missing from an attack on our convoy. Jed said they would wait for the gunship to head back down there armed and ready before they could check for survivors. Howard is rounding up a large force, and they should be ready by the time the gunship arrives. Sorry, but they won't have any update for four to five hours."

Jane and Ben left to go to their home, and Wes caught Joe off to the side. "Joe, several of the citizens, said they saw a truck heading away from the attack with three red headed girls and several young men. Two of the men were wounded. Joe, I'd lower expectations on any of our missing crew being seen again alive."

Joe was in a daze himself. He was very close to Cole and thought of him as a son. Joe was devastated and didn't know how to break the news to Cloe. Even though they weren't together, she still cared for him. He turned to go inside and saw Cloe and Cobie staring at him and Wes walking away. They saw the tears streaming down his cheeks.

Joe didn't wait until they heard from California. He looked through his box of Grandma's letters and found the one on the loss of a loved one. He had initially read this letter right after Madison was kidnapped. Joe prayed several times that Cole was still alive somewhere down in California and would walk up to Joe's front door one day to embrace Cloe and shake his hand.

Dear Joe:

It's now a year since you started reading my letters. You lost your best friend and me, and I hope you have recovered. I hope you have a new love interest in your life to care for you and to discuss things with you. One should never intentionally try to be alone. We are social animals and need other people. Shake off losses and work hard to move on in life but never forget the ones you love. I could say crap like "don't cry over spilt milk," but that doesn't make the pain of the loss go away. I can say that you have to man up and do what it takes to survive and prosper in this mean old world. Don't be a victim.

Love Grandma.

Molly Jenson and her younger cousins were herded toward the old cargo hanger and pushed into a large restroom with only one entrance. The guard pointed his rifle to the stalls. "Girls, you have a long flight ahead and only a five-gallon bucket to do your business on the plane. If I were you, I'd go now. You'll be leaving here in about twenty minutes."

The room stank of urine and human waste. The stench made Molly queasy, but she kept herself from vomiting. Life was tough since the grid went down, but life just got mean and nasty. Molly could only imagine what these men wanted them for and she vowed to kill herself before she would be passed around as a sex toy for these perverts.

Gemma whined, "Where are we going? Why can't you let us go?"

The guard laughed. "Shut up. I'm trying to be nice to you so shut up and go to the bathroom."

Molly placed her index finger over her mouth. "Shush. Don't make him mad. Those men shot up our convoy; they will kill you if you don't shut up. Do what these people say until we can figure out how to escape."

Jenny started crying and blubbering about life wasn't fair. "I want to go home. Why can't we go home?"

A rough looking woman wearing camo walked into the restroom. "Get your asses up and follow me to the plane. You have 2,000 miles to go before you get to your new FEMA job and home. The flight will make three stops along the way to drop off or pick up passengers to be relocated.

You ladies will end up in Kentucky and become farmers for our new government. You are damned lucky to be going to FEMA; we also sell to the sex traders. You will be helping to feed our troops and fellow workers. Here, take these MREs and four bottles of water for each of you. Don't guzzle the water down too quickly because you won't get more on this flight. Now get on the plane."

Molly walked up the steps that hung down from the back of the plane. The seats of the old DC3 had been stripped from the plane, and Molly saw dozens of men and a few women sitting or lying on the floor. As promised, there were six – five-gallon pails at the back of the plane. Molly looked for a spot for them away from the others and saw Cole lying on the floor with a bloody bandage on his head.

Molly walked over to Cole when another person almost stepped on his face. Molly dropped to her knees and slid her lap under Cole's head to help protect him. She pulled the bandage loose and saw the wounds were covered in dirt. Molly tore a piece from the bottom of her T-shirt and poured some of her water on the rag. She mopped the dirt away from the cut when a man forced his way between Gemma and Molly.

"Hey Babe, don't worry about him. He's going to the coal mines in Kentucky. He'll be dead in a couple of months. I'm a real man, and I can take care of you."

The stench from the man was almost overpowering. He reeked of tobacco, urine, and diesel fuel. Molly clenched her teeth. "Get your stinking ass away from us. This is my husband, and I'm going to take care of his wound. Go!"

"Hey, you'll sing a different tune in a few days after those farmers pass you around. I'll go find me a woman who appreciates a real man."

166

Molly tried to get comfortable with Cole's head in her lap and wondered what would happen to her and her cousins when the plane landed. She hated Cole for what his leader, Joe, had done to her father and mother, but she couldn't get herself to back away from helping a wounded man that had saved her life. She knew they were traitors, but they were still her parents.

The rough looking woman from the bathroom walked up the middle of the people threading her way to Molly. "Girl, if you care for him, you'd better get him to wake up quickly. They only pay us for the live healthy ones. He'll be dumped from the flight on the next leg if he's not awake and looking healthy by mid-flight."

Molly's voice was very soft and shaky at best. "Ma'am, will they keep my husband and me together with my sisters?"

"You girls are going to a farm in Kentucky, and your husband will go to the mines in Western Kentucky. Hon, you'll probably never see him again. Mention you are a family every chance you get, and some softhearted clerk might place you together. Sorry, we just find the volunteers and FEMA makes the rules on where they can best be used for the government's reconstruction effort."

Molly poured water on the rag, wiped his face again, and then shook him. He moved a little and groaned. She then poured water from one of his bottles on his head, and he began to wake up. A few minutes later, his eyes snapped open, and Molly placed her hand over his mouth. "Be quiet and wake up. They will kill you if you can't work. I told them you are my husband. I don't want those other men after me. We all have a chance of staying together."

167

Cole's vision was blurry but regained focus as he felt his face being washed. Her lap felt good against his face, and he gazed up into her bright green eyes. The gorgeous woman and flaming red hair that fell down beside his head were somehow keeping him calm when his mind was panicked. She was very tender as she cleaned his wounds. He smiled up at her but received a look of disgust in return. Cole remembered meeting her and wondered how he had pissed this woman off so much.

Every time he closed his eyes, she slapped his face and said, "Stay awake stupid if you want to live."

Cole very much wanted to live and find out why this angel was mad at him. The plane droned on for hours until it landed the first time during the long journey.

☆

Chapter 14

Ben watched Jane tend the garden and knew she was thinking about Cole. Her eyes were damp, and tear streaks were running down her cheeks. Jane had withdrawn into a shell for the first few months after Cole disappeared and it took all of Ben and Charlie's patience to deal with her emotional state. She had done better for the last several months as long as she kept busy and her mind off missing Cole.

They had a ceremony two months after Cole was pronounced dead and Ben placed a cross in one corner of their courtyard. Jane visited the cross every morning before breakfast and every night before she went to bed. Jane was praying for Cole one morning when Charlie walked up behind her. "Mom is it okay if Cloe and I take the Jeep over to the cabins to fish in the pond?"

Jane was pleased and smiled at Charlie, "Just take your gear and rifles. Son, always be prepared. And do I have to tell you to not do anything with Cloe that you wouldn't do in front of me."

"Mom, I'm not a child anymore. I'm 16 going on 17, and I'm responsible. Besides, Cloe is only my friend. I wish she cared for me, but she sees me as Cole's little brother. Don't worry so much."

Ben walked over a few minutes later. "Babe, what is Charlie up to today?"

"He and Cloe are going over to the pond to fish."

Ben laughed and spoke before he thought. "Is that what the kids call necking these days?"

Ben choked when he realized what he had said. "Babe, I'm sorry. I know Cloe was Cole's girl."

"Don't worry about that. It would be great if Cloe and Charlie get together."

Ben said, "Joe, and I plan to go to the bear cave in the morning. Last year we talked about using it to store some emergency supplies and forgot about it when the shit hit the fan. Joe is taking Cobie and Cloe, and I want you and Charlie to join us. We'll walk over, take a lunch with us, and then check out the cave."

The next morning they had breakfast at Joe's house and took off walking to the cave after they ate. They strolled along chatting as they proceeded through the forest stopping to observe the birds and flowers. The air was crisp and clean with only the usual pine smell. There were very few wood fires, so there was just a faint smell of smoke in the air. The birds grew silent as they passed but sang their songs up ahead.

Joe saw the ridge where the cave was located. "Now the going gets tough. We have to climb to midways of the ridge and begin working our way west just about where that pine tree sticks out at an angle. Then we go about 50 yards to the mouth of the cave. Cloe have your M14 ready for action if we see a bear. Jane, you and Cobie need to stay back. Your AR15s will only piss off a Grizzly."

Cloe protested. "Dad, we haven't seen another Grizzly around here since that one tried to eat poor Bennie."

"We just need to be prepared for any possible situation. You need to remember that every time you venture out. This isn't like a trip to the mall back in the day. We still have thugs and now have wild animals to contend with now. Ben and I will take the lead, and you four stay outside until we make sure it's safe," Joe replied.

The ridge was rocky but had moss growing everywhere in the shade. The moss made the going tough because it made the rocks slick and treacherous. They each slipped on the moss several times and suffered cuts and abrasions to their hands and knees. Joe felt stupid that none of them had thought to wear gloves except Cloe and Charlie.

"Dad, if you had been prepared you would have worn gloves like me. I even brought a pair for Charlie."

"Smart ass. I think you need a good spanking," Joe replied.

Charlie helped Cloe several times to keep her from slipping or falling. He was very attentive to her without being too obvious.

Joe saw the rock outcropping that concealed the mouth of the cave and pointed. "The mouth of the cave is behind that rock. Follow me."

Joe walked around the inside of the rock and was standing on a narrow path that led into the cave. "Get your guns ready and place your lights on your head. I'll go first and cover my front and right side. Ben, you cover to my left. The last time I was here was in the middle of the winter, and the Black Bears were thick as dog hair on the floor of the cave about thirty feet inside."

Joe sniffed the air and only noticed a weak smell of ammonia and urine. "I smell animal piss. Keep your eyes open."

Joe turned his light on and thought he saw a flicker of light for a minute up ahead and then nothing but darkness. Then he caught a whiff of smoke that became stronger as they walked deeper into the cave. Joe felt a draft on his neck and discovered that there was a breeze blowing into the cave. He knew there must be an opening to the surface at the back of the cave.

The odor of smoke grew stronger, then he smelled something very familiar. "Damn, someone is cooking rabbits over an open fire. I know that smell. Hey, is someone in here. We won't hurt you. I promise."

No one answered, but they heard feet scurrying in the darkness, and then they heard a baby crying. Joe repeated his words. "We're here to help you and won't hurt you. Come on out and talk with us."

"Billy, please talk with the man."

"No, Betty shut up."

The voices were from young kids. Then the sound of the baby filled the cave again. Joe was worried that whoever was in the cave might feel desperate and start shooting. "Okay, we're leaving and won't come back. Don't shoot."

Ben whispered to Joe, "I think it's some kids with a baby. They must have been abandoned. We can't leave them here alone. Let me get Jane to talk them into coming home with us."

Joe didn't like the idea but gave in to Ben. "Okay, but keep your gun ready."

Ben left and came back with Jane. Jane had Ben shine his light on her so the kids could see her. "Kids come on out to me. I'll fix you a nice hot supper and give you clean, warm beds to sleep in. We like children."

Before Jane finished speaking, they could hear feet hitting the cave floor. Jane saw a blur, and a tiny little girl bumped into Jane and wrapped her arms around Jane's legs.

"Mama, mama, your back," the little girl cried.

A young boy came out of the darkness carrying a baby. "Please don't hurt my sisters."

Jane took the baby boy from the lad. "Where are your parents?"

The boy whimpered. "Daddy was killed in Ashland a long time ago. Mommy brought us into the woods after he was killed. We found the cave before the snow and moved in. Mommy had to run off some scary animals with fire. Mommy left us to find food and didn't come back. I've been killing and cooking rabbits to keep from starving. The baby is sick."

Jane checked the infant. "How old is the baby?"

"His birthday was before mommy left."

Cloe and Cobie joined them in the cave and began caring for the children. They fed them the lunch they had brought for their picnic and then took them back to the Fort.

Zeke sent a nurse and doctor down from headquarters to examine the children and found them to be dehydrated, and malnourished but otherwise in good physical condition. Ben placed them in Cole's old bedroom and added an extra bed for the older boy. The baby slept in a bassinette in with Jane and Ben. The kids were Johnny, Betty, and the baby was named Kate. Their mom and dad were Katherine and Andy Miller, and they were on vacation from Missouri when the grid went down.

Ben and Joe went back to the cave, found their mother's journal, and found they had been living in the cave for over a year. They were too afraid to come out of the cave. Their father was killed by one of the gangs, and the mother barely escaped with the kids and the clothes on their backs. She had roamed the area stealing from Joe's community small amounts of food and a few rabbit traps to keep her kids from starving. Her fear cost her her life and almost killed the kids. Joe and his people would have gladly taken them in and fed them.

***

Later that week Cloe saw her mom hanging the wash on the line and saw something she hadn't noticed before. "Mom, not that it's any of my business, but has Joe noticed that you haven't had your period in months and you are putting on a bit of weight?"

Cobie placed her finger to her lips and shushed her daughter. "Cloe, yes, I'm going to have a baby. What you don't know is that a year after you were born I had a miscarriage and am frightened to death that I'll lose the baby. I wanted to get past three months before I told Joe."

"Mom, I'm sorry for your loss, and I wish you had told me sooner. I think it's great and I won't spoil your surprise. Can I ask a favor?"

"Sure darling."

"Don't name the baby Cole if it's a boy. I'm going to name my first boy after Cole."

Cloe broke into tears and ran back into the house.

****

175

Cobie, Joe, and Cloe went across the courtyard to Jane's to visit with her and see how the children were doing. Betty and Johnny were outside playing with several toy cars and trucks and ran over to Cobie when they arrived. Cobie picked up Johnny and Betty clung to Cloe. Jane came out to greet them with the baby in her arms. "I haven't cared for a baby in 15 years. My, this is a lot of work, but I love every minute of it. These children are so polite and well behaved."

Cloe asked, "Jane, are you going to keep the kids?"

Ben hugged Jane. "Jane and I want one of our own, but it's apparent that won't happen, so we prayed for a baby. God gave us three, and we can't separate them. It will be hard, but we hope some of our friends and neighbors might help from time to time."

Cobie reached out to cuddle Kate. "I'll be glad to be the aunt that spoils them and Cloe can be a big sister who teaches them how to be mischievous."

"I can do that. Charlie and I can teach them how to fish, trap, and raise a garden. We'll also teach them some kid's games," Cloe offered with a big laugh.

Joe held little Kate in his arms as Cobie refereed a fight over toys between Billy and Betty. He was amazed at how natural Cobie took to mothering the two energetic youngsters. They had more piss and vinegar than any five of the other children at the Fort. Joe had helped babysit the kids several times since Jane and Ben adopted them and thoroughly enjoyed the experience.

Joe saw Cobie walking toward him with a kid hanging around her waist. "Babe, I always wanted kids but going from zero to three would kill this old man. I don't see how Ben and Jane keep up with these little darlings."

"I know. I'm about pooped myself. I'll trade you these two for Kate so I can get some rest. They want to play hide and go seek, and you have to do the seeking so don't think you can run to the neighbors and hide in a hammock with a beer," Cobie warned.

Joe smirked as he handed Kate to Cobie. "You arrived just in time."

The fragrance hit her before she stuck her arms out. "On second thought I'll seek the kids while you change the poopy diaper. Remember to use the white cream stuff on her rash."

"That's not fair. You said you wanted her," Joe protested.

Before Cobie could answer, Cloe and Charlie walked into the courtyard and began to play hide and seek with the kids.

Cobie waved and said, "Cloe keep them busy for a while. Joe, and I need to talk for a few minutes."

Cloe winked at her mom and then whispered to Charlie. "Mom is about to tell Dad that she is pregnant. I can't wait to see how he reacts."

Cobie and Joe took the baby to the bathroom, and Joe changed the stinky kid under Cobie's watchful eye. "Joe you are very good with the baby. Does keeping Kate ever make you want one of your own?"

Joe fastened the last diaper pin. "Yes, it does. I am happy with my family and would never push you, but I love kids and would like one of my own. You know I love Cloe, but I guess it's not quite the same as seeing your own child born and then raise them."

"So if I became pregnant, you would be happy? Cobie asked.

Joe turned, took Cobie in his arms, and kissed her. "Of course, I'd be happy. Please don't have twins or triplets. Honestly, we haven't been too careful lately, and I kinda hoped you were trying to get pregnant."

Cloe laughed and hugged Joe tight. "Well, I can't get pregnant now, so we don't need to be careful."

"Babe, you mean we can never have a child?" Joe asked with emotion.

"No silly, we are going to have a baby and women can't get pregnant when they are already pregnant,' Cobie exclaimed.

"You mean ..."

Yes, silly, you are going to be a father in 5-6 months. I'm going to see the doc next week to pin down a delivery date."

Joe hugged and kissed Cobie several times, and then lifted her T-shirt and kissed her belly several times. He introduced himself to his child and began talking to it as though it were sitting in front of him.

For the next two weeks Joe told everyone, he met that he was going to be a father. He was on cloud nine and felt good about life. Most of the criminals and thugs had been killed or run off months ago. They had plenty of food, water, and proper shelter, so life was good now. Joe knew there were more threats and opportunities still to be dealt with but nothing that scared him. It was as good a time as possible to have a new baby.

☆

Chapter 15

April 2040 **Two years after the SHTF**

Joe's eyes snapped to attention, the noise was deafening. The smell was overpowering, and his foggy mind tried to decide to stand and fight or flee. Suddenly he felt a stabbing pain in his ribs.

A worn out Cobie elbowed her husband. "Joe, get your ass out of bed and check Josh's diaper and feed him. I'm about to pass out from the odor so count on a messy diaper. You knocked me up, and half of this baby thing is yours."

Joe rubbed the sand from his eyes and wobbled as he slowly moved his feet to the floor. "Babe, I'm sorry, but I'm moving slow. Pounding T-posts and stringing more fences to extend our plowed ground about killed me."

Cobie laughed and rolled over to Joe. "Hon, if you hadn't pounded me that day without protection we wouldn't be parents with a shitty diaper to change."

Joe slapped his wife on the butt. "If I remember correctly, you didn't exactly put up a fight, and I remember you hollering ..."

"Shut up. Cloe might hear you. Now clean up that dirty boy and feed him. It's your turn, and I'm going back to sleep."

"But we love Josh."

Cobie rolled back over and answered from under the covers. "I love him a lot more when you get up at two in the morning to feed him and change shitty diapers."

Joe picked up his two-month-old son and walked to the kitchen to heat some water to warm the baby bottle. He tried not to take a breath until he'd cleaned up the mess and had a fresh diaper on the kid.

Cloe came from her room into the kitchen yawning. "Dad, go back to bed, you're too old for this. I'll feed my little brother so you can get some sleep."

"Baby Girl, have I told you how much I love you?" Joe replied with his eyes barely open.

"Dad, stop the Baby Girl shit. I'm too old for that. That's the first time in a year you called me that."

Joe handed Josh to Cloe and marveled at how much the two looked alike. "That poor boy is going to be hairy just like your Mom and you. I hope he is at least tall like me. We don't need a midget Harp in the family."

"Dad, shut up and go to bed. You're not funny and couldn't earn a dime as a comedian. Go to bed. I got this."

Joe gave Cloe a kiss on the forehead. "Thanks, hon, I'm beat. I guess you didn't sleep much last night."

Cloe's red tear filled eyes gave her grief away. It was just over a year since the convoy had been attacked and Cole disappeared with Butch and the people that were to join the community. They had searched the area off and on for several months and only managed to get into several bloody battles with the slaver gang before finally wiping them out.

Cloe tried to speak, but the words didn't come to her lips. Joe joined her on the couch, placed his arm around her, and kissed her on the forehead. "Honey, it's time to move on. I know it's not something you want to hear, but it's been a year. Either Cole is dead, or they flew him to the East Coast. In either case, he is dead to us forever now. Baby, there are several boys that like you and ... well, damn, you need to move on."

Cloe sniffed and wiped the tears away on Joe's shoulder. "Dad, I know what you are saying, but I always thought Cole and I would be married in a few years and have babies on our own. I've been in denial for a year now thinking Cole would walk through the door anytime. I now know he is dead.

Holding little Josh makes me want a couple of my own. Dad, give me a bit longer, and I'll get back in the game. I know I haven't been pulling my weight. Oh, Charlie asked me to go fishing with him again today. Do you think that will bother Jane or Ben? I would never do anything to hurt them."

Joe smiled and stroked her hair. "I'm sure Jane and Ben would be pleased that you and Charlie spend time together. Do you want me to say something to Jane?"

"Please feel her out. Charlie and I get along okay but have to sneak around to see each other for fear of upsetting Jane. We don't have the same kind of feelings that Cole and I had, but I like him a lot. I need a good friend. Losing Emily and Cole last year hurt me deeply."

Joe went back to bed while Cloe took the now warm milk to the living room and curled up with her little brother on the recliner. The truth was that Cloe couldn't sleep and was a wreck. Cole had disappeared a year ago. She would never forget him because he was her first love even though she was fourteen when he disappeared. Cloe went through shock, denial, and grieving for over nine months before she could function normally again. Helping her mother through her pregnancy forced her to function day to day, but she lay awake most nights crying for Cole until little Josh was born. The baby gave her a reason to live again.

Joe talked with Jane the next day, and she was delighted about Charlie and Cloe seeing each other. "Joe, we saw this coming months ago. The two have been by each other's side since Cole died. They help console each other and cry on the other's shoulder. Charlie kept his grief inside, and it would have eaten him up if not for Cloe. I just don't want him to feel guilty that he ended up with his brother's girlfriend."

Later that night Joe read one of his Grandma's last letters.

Dear Joe:

Joe, your Dad and Mom came to visit today. They surprised me and just popped in on me. They came up to vacation in Bandon, and your old man wanted to play at Bandon Dunes and Pacific Dunes. I had Alfred make a few calls and got him and your mom T-times. Your Mom and Dad visited with me the rest of the day before driving over to the resort. We had a great time, and the only downside was that you didn't come with them. I hope that you come see me before I kick the bucket. Remember you can't drown all your sorrows in beer.

Yes, your Dad told me that you were drinking too much since what's her name died. Forget the turd and find a good woman. If you fall off a horse, you dust yourself off and climb back in the saddle. Not that a woman is like a horse ... oh shit, you know what I mean.

Now the fun stuff. I made Alfred take me up to Bandon, and I played the front nine with your folks. I don't have much strength to hit a long drive, but by God, I can chip and putt better than your Dad or your Mom. I took them for a dollar for eight out of nine holes from a hundred yards into the green. Your Dad thinks he's a good golfer but his game stinks. The dummy was using a range detector for 50-yard shots and missing the green by 15 yards.

He putted from fifteen feet and was five feet short on number 7. I told him, "Pull your thong out of your ass, Alice." He got red in the face and gave me the bird. I should have spanked him, but I was laughing too hard. Your Mom will give him hell later for abusing his dear old mother.

I asked your Dad and Mom to move out here and take over the operation, but your old man is almost as stubborn as his dad was. Your mom also laid the law down and wouldn't move away from Nashville. Your Mom and I don't get along very well, but I hope I hid that from you.

I know neither of you needs my money, and I really believe you both think money can't buy happiness but believe me purchasing nice toys is fantastic. I bought a bunch of Go Karts for the kids in the neighborhood and pissed the police off. I paid the kid's fines and built them a track over by the north pasture.

Okay, I'm rambling as usual. I can't wait for your call tomorrow. Have a good life.

Love Grandma

Joe stopped to think back at the awkward moments during the holidays when his Grandma and his mom didn't get along. He was usually outside playing, but as he got older, he knew his Mom didn't like his Grandma because she always made nasty comments about his Grandma. He loved his mom but had a hard time liking her because she also treated his dad poorly.

☆

Chapter 16

July 2045 **Seven years after TSHTF**

Cloe woke in the middle of the night very tired and bleary eyed for lack of sleep the past four days. Little Cole was in bed with her, and Charlie was not in their bed. Cole had a cold and felt miserable. Cloe was worn out from taking care of him and the new baby. She thanked God for her mom and Jane, her mother-in-law, for helping take care of baby Cole while she was pregnant and when little Emily was born. The baby would be a month old tomorrow. Cole turned a year old last month and was a handful.

The old windup clock showed 3:00 am so she guessed her husband was up feeding and changing the baby. She slid out of bed leaving her munchkin sound asleep. Cloe tiptoed into the family room to find Charlie asleep on the couch with their new baby on his chest sound asleep. She bent over and kissed her husband and precious little Emily.

Charlie peeked between weary eyelids. "Good morning beautiful. Why don't you go back to bed? I've got Emily taken care of."

Cloe forced a smile from her tired face. "Babe, I don't think I can get up. Thank God, your mom is keeping the kids while we drive over to the coast. I need to relax on the beach. Joan tells me the ocean is beautiful and go figure there aren't any crowds anymore. I haven't swum in anything but our pond since I was a kid."

Charlie looked wistfully at Cloe and wanted some alone time with her. Going from boyfriend and lover to having two babies wasn't the best for their love life. Charlie loved his life with Cloe and doted on the kids; however, a break was what they both needed. "I need to work a few hours with your Dad, but you can count on me to be with you most of the time. I hope the wind doesn't blow sand in our faces all day. That darn wind off the ocean can be rough. Did you pick up a swimsuit for us?"

Cloe laughed, and her face lit up. "Grandma Harp's home is right on the beach, and I'll be there if you are looking for me. I'll be the one rocking the white Bikini. Mom will have a yellow Bikini. Don't you stare at her if you want to keep your eyes!"

"Beautiful, I only have eyes for you. I do want to get a very close up view of you in that Bikini and perhaps without it. We need a plan to send your folks out to play by themselves," Charlie proposed.

Cloe blew Charlie a kiss. "Babe, Mom, and I already have a plan for us to be away a while and them to be away from the house for a while. Josh was a handful and has worn Mom down almost as much as my brats have worn us down. Joe is a good father, but he doesn't help as much as you do around the house. I tell Mom that I trained you better. Damn, I can't wait to leave after we drop the kids off."

Charlie's eyes were closed as he mumbled. "I'm looking forward to the trip myself and being alone with you for a change. Remember, Joe, and I are going to check out a couple of boats that Jed told us might fit into our long-term plans. Wes has experience on fishing boats, and we hope to get several running and augment our food supply. Joe is also going to check on the salt plant. Their output has been off for several months."

Charlie fell back asleep, and Cloe slumped down into her favorite recliner and wondered where the years had gone. She replayed the last five years in her mind and mostly had a smile. There were mainly good times even in the year after the world ended. Hard times brought people together, and people tend to forget most of the bad times.

She was 12-years-old when her mom and she fled to the mountains. Joe married her mom when she was 13, and she fell in love with Cole that year. A year later, Cole was killed or disappeared down in California when she was 14. She started dating Charlie, and to no one's surprise, they fell in love a year later. They had dated for several years when Cloe became nauseous every morning. She was four months along during the wedding and didn't care what anyone thought. She felt lucky to have had two men that she loved with all her heart.

Charlie was a bit shorter than Cole but just as broad in the shoulders and fearless. He was every bit as good a soldier as Cole but much smarter concerning strategy and tactics. He thought things through before reacting and was a blessing to Joe and Wes in keeping the community safe.

Cloe looked around the small family room. It was about 16 feet wide by 15 feet long and was the end of two shipping containers that had the sides cut out. Her whole house was made out of shipping containers. The house wouldn't win any Good Housekeeping awards, but it was very safe and functional. The container house community had grown over the past five years and now had three large complexes much more extensive than their original Fort. There were 20-25 homes in each unit, and each house had a lovely courtyard for gardens and kids to play. They also had several walled in open areas that the entire community shared for extensive gardens, picnics, and fun. One was large enough to play football or baseball. Everything planned or built since the grid went down was based on safety and function before aesthetics.

Charlie stirred and opened his bleary eyes to see his beautiful wife. He never told Cloe, but he had secretly been jealous of Cole. Charlie kissed her on the cheek and placed the baby in the crib. He then took a shower and started making breakfast for Cobie and Joe before they left that morning.

The drive to Bandon took about three hours in Joe's Suburban. Wes and Charlie had reworked the engine and replaced all of the electronics with undamaged parts found in shipping containers. The containers made great Faraday cages, and there were millions of full shipping containers across the USA. Many had ATVs, motorcycles, and a few had complete vehicles that were being shipped in and out of the country. The ones with auto parts were the ones that Zeke's crew sought out so they could get cars and trucks back in operation.

Charlie watched the hills and trees fly by as Joe sped northwest between Myrtle Point and Coquille on Highway 42. The road wound along the river valley as it marched its way to Coquille where they would take 42 South to the coast and Bandon.

Charlie worked up the courage to speak. "Joe, I know Zeke's Chief of Staff told you it was safe up in Bandon, but I'm not convinced. One of the Canadian refugees told me that there was a mean gang up in Seattle that was capturing slaves for the eastern part of the USA. He said that he heard this was common across Canada and the USA and that rogue parts of both the Canadian and US Governments were behind the capture of slaves."

Joe heard some rumors along the same lines a week ago but was confident Bandon was safe. "I think we will be safe enough, although it never hurts to be on guard. Everyone brought their combat gear, weapons, and a basic combat load of ammo, so we're as prepared as possible. Dan's team has guards posted around Bandon, so we should be in great hands. I guess it wouldn't hurt to keep our rifles with us even at the beach and restaurant. The Israelis had to do that all the time due to the constant threat from the Muslim extremists."

Cobie reached back from the front seat and poked Cloe. "We have to visit with Joan and see their children. I also hear that Peggy is visiting up here with little Butch. It's a shame she never remarried."

"Mom, don't bring up anything that would upset her. She still hasn't recovered," Cloe said.

Charlie squeezed his wife's hand. "We'll always miss our loved ones, but life has to move on. I pray that most of the fighting is done but not a day goes by that we don't hear about those groups in the east with their slave factories, mines, and farms. If they continue to grow, they will attack us one day."

Cobie knew that Joe was sick and tired of fighting even though the past three years had been relatively quiet. "Joe, I hate to say it, but Charlie is right. Even though we have a great life here in Southern Oregon, the rest of the country has pockets of organized slave camps. I don't care if they are called FEMA camps, they couldn't possibly have been set up by our legitimate government."

Joe's temples pounded as the blood surged through his veins. He could hear his heartbeat in his ears. "Let's concentrate on having a good time at the beach and can all this fighting and slave talk wait until we go back home next week? For once, we need to rest and relax. Please."

A hush fell over the vehicle and then suddenly Cloe laughed. "Dad, we will enjoy this weekend and shut up about what you don't want to hear, but only until next Monday morning when Charlie and I camp out on your head until you listen to us."

Joe knew his hardheaded daughter would worry him to death. "Agreed, there will not be any more discussion of work until Monday morning, and I promise to listen."

Cloe grinned and patted her dad's shoulder. "That's a deal. Charlie, will I look good in my Bikini with a shoulder holster?"

"You would be beautiful wearing anything. Hey, that's 42 South. We're almost there."

The time flew, and they soon stopped at the checkpoint at Bear Creek Road, which was about three miles from the center of town. The two guards waved. "Hello, Mr. Harp. Dan said that you were due this morning. Please enjoy your stay in beautiful Bandon."

Charlie stuck his head out the window. "Have you seen anything suspicious or perhaps any strangers down here lately?"

One of the guards replied. "Nothing suspicious but we have seen several groups of refugees traveling down Highway 101. They all said they were heading south to a warmer climate. Enjoy your visit."

Joe drove straight to his Grandma's house on the beach without stopping to visit with Dan or Joan as had been hinted. Joe was on a mission to relax, drink beer, and watch his wife sunbathe from under an umbrella. Bandon wasn't hot on a pleasant summer's day, and the wind blew most days from the ocean. The summer was especially warm, and the daytime temperatures were in the mid-80's.

The home was about two miles south of Bandon and was a five-bedroom rustic house built to mimic a Victorian mansion. It was the only three-story home for miles on the beachfront. Joe had been there many times when he was growing up but only once recently. It actually belonged to Alfred who had been his Grandma's butler and secret lover. He cared for her for many years.

"Let's drop the luggage off in the rooms, eat one of the sandwiches we brought with us and collapse on the beach," Cobie proposed.

Joe picked their luggage up and headed up the stairs. "Come on hussy, I want to see you in that bathing suit."

They dressed in their swimwear and were back down on the patio eating sandwiches and guzzling beer thirty minutes later. The gulls shrieked above their heads, and the wind whistled as it blew through the patio. The air smelled both salty and fresh, which was a smell Charlie wasn't used to. Jane only took them to the beach every few years when they were kids. They camped a lot, but she couldn't afford Bandon's high prices as a single mother of two sons.

The wind was gentle for Bandon, and the sun was warm, so everyone except Charlie fell asleep quickly lying on towels placed on the sand. Charlie walked back up to the patio and scanned the beach and area around him with his binoculars. There was one couple on the beach about a half-mile north of them and two men fishing several hundred yards south, but no threats could be seen.

Later Charlie saw a small ship sitting still in the water about a mile northwest of the house and felt that he was being watched. He caught the glint of sunlight being reflected from the boat back to him. He walked out to the Suburban and brought two of their sniper rifles into the house through the garage so no one on the boat could see him.

He placed the Barrett M107 on the table by the window and sighted the boat in with his spotter's scope. He about crapped when he saw a man behind a large telescope and even worse there was a deck mounted .50 caliber machine gun. The man was actually scanning the south end of Bandon and taking notes. There were several people on deck dressed like soldiers, and he saw two large Zodiacs tied to the back of the ship.

Charlie went to Joe's room and used Joe's walkie-talkie to call Dan. "Dan, come in Dan."

"Charlie is that you?"

"Yes, it's me, Charlie. Dan, has anyone reported a ship about a half mile due west of the city that is surveilling the city?"

"Why yes, the captain of the ship came ashore to purchase supplies several days ago. He said they were having engine trouble and would have it repaired in a few days."

Charlie was now very concerned. "Hey, by any chance has anyone been reported missing?"

"None of our people but a man came into town this morning and said some men raided their camp up at Bandon Dunes and shot up their camp and kidnapped a dozen people. The man was drunk, so we didn't pay him much mind."

"I'm wondering if we should increase our guards and be ready for trouble. I used my spotter scope to watch the ship, and they have a big assed telescope watching the town. They also have a Ma Deuce mounted on the front deck. They are up to something and could be trouble," Charlie said.

Dan didn't put much stock in any kidnapping but agreed to increase the guards before they ended the conversation. Charlie hooked the solar charger to the walkie-talkie and left it on the patio table so he could hear if anyone called. Then he took his spotter's scope and his AR down to the beach and plunked down next to Cloe.

Cloe was only a few feet from her mom, and their faces were covered by big floppy hats. He tried to see if he could tell them apart and except for the different colored bathing suits and the bullet wound scar on Cobie's shoulder, their bodies were identical. Both were five feet nothing tall, had thick dark hair on their arms, and the same voluptuous body. Charlie couldn't help but think that Cloe would only get more gorgeous as she ages.

Cloe woke up a few hours later and walked toward the water with Charlie following her. "Babe, I have to pee so you might want to stay away for a minute."

"Darn, you are a common old girl aren't you? I'm surprised you don't dip snuff and spit on the sidewalks."

Cloe motioned him to come to her with her finger. He walked away from her and moved into deeper water, Cloe followed him and then motioned for him again. Charlie slid his arms around her to hug her. She jumped up on him and knocked him down into the cold water. She tried to hold him down under the water, but he picked her up, slung her over his shoulder, and carried her to the beach.

Cobie woke up and saw Charlie packing Cloe over his shoulder. "I remember when Joe could carry me on his shoulder, but I think old age is catching up to him."

Charlie gently laid Cloe on her towel and lay on top of her kissing and biting her neck. Cobie looked over at the lovebirds. "Either you two need to go to your room, or Joe and I do. If Joe wakes up, he'll throw a bucket of water on you."

"Mom, roll over and mind your business. Charlie is just kissing .... Oh, damn that feels so good. Come on Charlie let's go up to our room now."

That was Charlie's first mistake that evening. He forgot to keep watch on the ship. The second was not telling Joe about the ship and the man watching the city with the telescope. The third was not mentioning the machine gun.

Cobie watched the kids leave and run up to the house in their haste and began kissing Joe on his stomach. Soon everyone who should have been watching for danger was involved in hanky-panky and didn't notice the two Zodiacs head to the beach just south of the town.

Two hours later Joe was grilling steaks on the grill as the sun went down in the west. The red streaks blended in with the blue and white sky yielding a beautiful sunset. The women were baking potatoes and making a salad up in the kitchen. The hickory smoke and steak's aroma were making Charlie's mouth water. Charlie brought Joe a cold brew and remembered the conversation with Dan. "Joe, Dan told me this afternoon that a man reported that his camp had been attacked and a dozen people were kidnapped along with a couple killed. I've been watching a ship floating about a half mile west of town, and I think they are up to no good."

Joe frowned and shrugged. "Did he call you on the radio?"

"No, I called him because I saw a man on that ship watching the town through a large telescope. Look over that way. See the light. That's the ship. I think it is a slave ship," Charlie said as he filled Joe in on the rest of his observations.

Joe pondered what to say when they heard the faint sound of an engine coming from the ocean. Joe said, "Don't move and stay calm. They can see us but can't hear us yet.

Hey, Cobie, I need both of you to sneak our rifles down here. We have our pistols. I think we are about to have some company. Move slowly and come back like nothing is going on. They are about 200 yards away."

"Joe, I'm sorry I didn't speak up earlier."

"Charlie, you did speak up, I just didn't listen. We need to capture one or two of these pricks and find out what is going on. They expect to have an easy time capturing us, but they are going to run into some bad luck."

The girls came back with the rifles tucked under some towels and lay them down beside the men. Joe said, "Girls go back in the house grab your weapons and more ammo. Low crawl back and take up defensive positions. I'm going to draw them in and then spring the trap. I need at least one alive."

Charlie could see the men sneaking along in the beach grass behind some shrubs. "Joe they're about fifty yards away."

"Let me know when they are fifty feet."

Charlie kept acting as if he was chugging his beer as he watched the men out of the corner of his eye. "Joe they will be about fifty feet by the time you bring your rifle up."

Joe reached down beside his leg and suddenly dropped to a kneeling position behind the brick patio wall and shot the first man his sights came across. The men were caught by surprise but quickly returned fire on Joe. Bullets struck the patio wall and shattered the glass windows on the house. Glass shards flew like missiles.

Charlie duplicated Joe's move but took a second more and shot his target in the right calf. The 5.56 bullet destroyed the man's knee, and he dropped writhing in agony. A bullet hit the house behind Charlie and ricocheted back hitting Charlie on the side. It was only a small fragment from the shot, but it stung like a hornet sting and caused Charlie to shoot high over the men's heads.

Cobie and Cloe fired several times from behind the far right patio wall, and all four of the men were down. The girls had more time to choose their targets, which resulted in one dead, one dying, and two that could talk.

Charlie and Joe took the men's weapons, drug the two that could talk to the patio wall, and propped them up. Joe stuck his rifle butt on the gaping wound on the knee of one of the men. "Does that hurt?"

"Of course it hurts moron."

Joe tapped him on the head with the butt of his rifle and then pointed the muzzle at the man's mouth. "Did that also hurt? I'd watch my mouth if I were you. Now if you want the pain to stop, you'll tell us what you were doing here and who do you work for?"

"Screw you and the horse you rode in on."

Joe butt stroked the man in the balls and then lifted his head with the barrel of the rifle while Charlie kept the other two guarded. "This is your last chance. Hey, you other two scumbags. If he doesn't answer my next question, I'm going to shoot his ear off. I will be questioning you also, and I don't have a lot of time."

The man saw the rifle pointed at the side of his head and then felt the cold steel against his cheek. "Okay, I'll talk. We are independent slavers who cover the northwest and sell to the highest bidder. We were going to sell you to FEMA for laborers."

Joe grinned and pulled the rifle back. "Now that's a good start. How many men are on the ship and are there any other Zodiacs?"

"There are 32 not counting this group, and there are two more boats. They are aground north of the city picking up slaves right now."

"How many slaves are on that ship?"

"We have captured 89 so far and plan to head down to Southern California to fly them to the Midwest for farms, factories, and mines. Some of the best looking women and young boys are sold to the sex traders. Hey, man, do you think we like doing this? We were starving up in Portland when we were captured and made to find slaves."

Joe shot the man square between the eyes and turned to shoot the others. Charlie aimed his rifle at one of the punks. "Do you have anything to add to that scumbag's information?"

The man spoke some drivel and Charlie shot the last two. "Joe, shouldn't we drive into town and help them?"

"Yes, that was going to be the next thing out of my mouth. Ladies, get dressed for war," Joe ordered.

Fifteen minutes later Joe was speeding toward Bandon on Highway 101. He headed for the north end of town where he thought the slavers staged their attack on the city. He made the sweeping turn through the city at full speed when the truck was strafed by bullets. Joe quickly yanked the steering wheel and drove the Suburban through the front window of an abandoned gift shop about a hundred yards from the docks.

They were protected from the gunfire, and Joe checked on the others. "Did anyone get hit?"

Cloe was frantically working on Charlie. "Charlie will live, but he took one from the side into his shoulder. I'm keeping pressure on the wound, but he needs a doctor now. I got hit by glass and only have minor cuts. Thank God our babies weren't in the truck."

Cobie had her weapon ready and visually swept the outside area behind the gaping hole in the front of the building. "I'm okay. Something hit me on my ass. I guess it was a bullet or fragment. Joe, take a look at my ass and make sure I'm okay."

Joe kept watching through the hole for threats while working around the vehicle to get to his wife. He tugged her pants down enough to see the top of her right butt cheek. "Babe your butt is still beautiful, but it has a piece of a bullet lodged about a half inch deep. Bite on something while I remove it."

Cobie grunted loudly even with her teeth clamped down on a rolled up shirtsleeve. "Honey, did you get it out?"

"Yes, and the wound isn't bleeding too bad. I'm squirting some wound seal into it and covering it with an antibiotic. Keep pressure on it, "Joe said.

Suddenly several bullets tore up the inside of the shop. Cloe and Joe returned fire and killed one of the men rushing the building. Cobie knew they would all die if Joe and Cloe weren't turned loose to fight. "Joe pull Charlie over here so I can keep pressure on his wound and he can do the same for me."

Joe pulled Charlie over to his wife. "Cloe and I have to go fight the bad guys. Charlie, hold this compress on my wife's butt, and Cobie, hold this compress on Charlie's shoulder."

Cobie joked with her son in law. "Put your hand on my ass and stop the bleeding. Now don't roam around back there or I'll shoot you in your other shoulder."

Cloe yelled back to them from the front of the store window. "Keep your clothes on while Dad and I go kick some ass. Keep your pistols handy. Well, Mom, keep your free hand handy. Charlie has your butt cheek in his good hand."

Cloe followed Joe out the back door, and they ran down the alley past the next building in an attempt to flank the enemy slavers. Joe stopped behind a truck and pointed. "There are two there and another behind that sign. I'll take out the two; you kill the one behind the sign."

Joe took aim, squeezed the trigger twice, and the men fell to the ground. Joe shot twice more to make sure they were dead. At the same time, Cloe saw her target lift his head to take a shot at the gift shop, and Cloe placed a bullet into his brain. Blood, bone, and gore hit the side of the building and splashed back on the sign. All three men were dead, so Joe ran to the gift shop and told Cobie that he and Cloe were going head hunting.

There was sporadic gunfire coming from the dock and the shops south along the waterfront. They slinked along the street a block away from the wharf to get into position. Joe helped Cloe climb to the rooftop of a restaurant across the street from the docks. They had an excellent view of the attacking force and could see their friends were pinned down in a small restaurant across the street on the pier.

Cloe didn't have her fancy wind meter or range detector, so she licked her thumb and felt the wind. As usual, it was blowing from the west, so it was in her face. The breeze was slight, and the yardage was only about 90 yards to the farthest target down to 25 for the closest. "Dad, I'll take the ones behind the cars to the left, and you take the ones down below us. This is like shooting fish in a barrel. I'll shoot on a count of three."

"One ... two ... three." Cloe and Joe opened fire on the men. Joe's targets had zero cover, and he killed the three of them quickly. Cloe got one in the head splattering brains on the woman next to him and then dropped the woman with a shot to her chest when she freaked out and tried to wipe the brains from her face. The other two scrambled under a truck. "Dad, I have two pinned down under that red Dodge truck. Be ready to shoot them when they crawl out."

Cloe aimed for the concrete a foot before the side of the truck and shot four times. One of the men quickly crawled out from under the truck but was slow to throw his guns down to the ground. Joe's bullet tore through his ear and blasted his jaw to smithereens. The man fell dead. Cloe shot twice more before Joe yelled, "Hon, I think you bounced one or two bullets into the bastard. Let's climb down and check him out, and then we'll hook up with our friends."

Cloe looked out to sea to find the ship. "Dad, the ship has moved closer to the mouth of the Coquille River. I think it's about a mile away and stopped for now. Do you think it can cause any trouble?"

"Hon, I don't know, but I guess we'll have to expect anything. The ship is probably waiting to dock after the raiding party reports the natives are subdued. There must be a larger raiding party at the dock and north of town."

☆

Chapter 17

The man under the truck was full of lead, and Joe left him where he lay. They ran back to the shop to help Cobie and Charlie. Joe carefully walked into the shop. "Charlie, is Cobie still bleeding or do you just like playing with my wife's butt?"

Cobie shushed Charlie. "I kinda like a young stud groping my butt every now and then. Charlie has been a gentleman and checked several times to make sure the bleeding stopped. It has, but I liked the feel and made him keep his hand there."

Cloe was behind Joe and saw her husband's red face, so she piled on. "So you like my Mom's butt more than mine. Do I need to squat down beside her and pull my pants down so you can compare?"

Charlie not to be buffaloed spoke up. "Cloe that's an excellent idea but don't you need to send Joe out on an errand just in case I choose the one I like best."

Cloe laughed. "Touché Charlie, finally after several years you can dish it out. Dad, try to back the truck out without jack knifing the trailer, and I'll clean the glass out so we can move these two perverts before I have a stepson stepbrother. Damn, that sounds kinda icky."

Joe fired the Suburban up and backed it over the rubble and out to the street. Cloe found a broom and a dustpan and swept the glass from the seats and the luggage area behind the seats. They carried Cobie to the back seat and let her slump down sideways to protect her wound. They took Charlie to the back of the vehicle and laid him on a pillow to keep him comfortable.

Before they could pull away and find their friends, Dan and several of his troops appeared. "Joe, are you okay?"

"I'm fine, but Cobie and Charlie need a doctor."

Dan saw Charlie and shook his hand. "All of the men who landed are dead, and I think we are safe now. My guys and the town folk massacred about a dozen north of town when they landed. I have someone watching the ship in case they try to send another wave of soldiers. Charlie, thanks for alerting us to the danger. You saved a bunch of lives."

Joe looked out to sea with his spotter's scope and saw the ship outlined by the setting sun. "That ship is parked about a half mile from the mouth of the river. I don't see any small boats and don't think the ship can do any damage, but my gut reaction is they will try to dock when they think they have subdued us. Get some men to the dock, and we'll pick them off before they can dock."

Charlie had an aha moment. "No, Joe, they have a deck mounted Ma Deuce. They will rip us apart. Take the Barrett and use the High Explosive (HE) shells to blow the machine gun up before they tear us apart."

Joe looked pissed and growled. "How long have you known ... Oh, well, we'll have that discussion later. Dan, have someone help me by carrying the ammo down to the dock."

Joe ran as fast as he could carry the heavy Barret .50 caliber sniper rifle. Cloe fetched her M14 sniper rifle and matched him step for step running to Dan's truck. Dan took off up 1st Street and worked his way to the Bandon South Jetty County Park where Joe and Cloe set up their rifles on top of the closest house. Joe chose the house because using the berm for cover wouldn't work because the blast of the high caliber weapon would shower them with dirt and sand.

The ship had moved closer to shore. What they saw made the hairs on the back of Joe's neck stand on end, and his stomach get queasy. The Ma Deuce was manned, and there was a crew removing a tarp from over a small cannon. Joe looked at Dan and passed the spotter's scope to him. "Joe, I think that is a 40 mm Bofors antiaircraft cannon. If they have enough shells, they can level Bandon."

Joe had a confused look on his face. "What is a Bofors and how bad can a small cannon be?"

"Joe, that's the same cannon the US Military uses on the AC-130 XZ Super Spectre gunship. That cannon can take out an army tank, blow big holes in buildings, and shoot down aircraft. It's bad."

Joe raised the Barret and took aim. "Cloe, you take the Ma Deuce, and I'll take the Bofors. They are about 1,500 yards from the mouth of the river. I don't think they will fire on the city until they have direct sight of our dock. The bastards will try to go up the river. I think they might be able to make it to the dock. Shit, I just don't know the draft of the ship or when the Coast Guard dredged the mouth the last time."

Dan interrupted. "Assume they can steam up the channel to the dock."

Joe changed his plan. "If I were them, I would get as close as possible to destroy our ships first and then worry about any soldiers. They will wait until they are inside the mouth of the river and begin firing when they can't travel any further to get maximum kill power from their machine gun.

Dan, spread your men out on this side of the river with every rifle they have and get ready to blast the decks of that ship. Once the ship reaches in the channel, it won't be more than 200 yards from your guys. Have your men rain hell on them, but only after Cloe and I fire our first shots.

Cloe and I can maybe get off three to four shots each before they zero in on us and blow this house and us sky high. The good news is our shots will only be from 300 – 400 yards. We won't miss our targets.

Dan, have a spotter directing your fire. Aim high to start and adjust. I'll shoot all of my HE rounds at the Bofors, pray for a hit on the cannon or the cannon's magazine. That might take out the crew along with the cannon, and I'll then switch to the MA Deuce. Cloe can quickly kill the man manning the machine gun, but they can quickly replace him.

Dan, I only have five HE rounds then the rest are armor piercing. They'll tear the hell out of anything they hit, but only a lucky shot would take out the cannon at this range. I only have a dozen armor piercing rounds."

The ship moved slowly to the mouth of the river and then slowed to a crawl. Joe looked over at Cloe. "They're going slow so they can read the depth of the river bottom. See that white post there, I'll shoot when the bow passes the post. I want you to shoot when I do. Don't stop until I say so. Girl, be ready to unass this roof if you see them train either gun on us. If they move either barrel this way jump off the roof and run like hell to that mansion up the hill."

Joe kissed Cloe on the forehead and sent her to the other end of the house. The ship was 50 yards from Joe's marker post and barely creeping. He saw the men get excited and one man stepped into the gunner's position. The barrel of the cannon began to rise. Joe knew he couldn't wait, aimed at the base of the cannon just below the magazine, and pulled the trigger.

The bullet hit the frame of the cannon and exploded sending shrapnel into the crew. The gunner and loader fell to the deck mortally wounded. The rest of the crew dragged the men from the cannon and tried to fill their slots. Joe squeezed the trigger again, and the explosion only damaged the cannon's mount. Several men and women were now pointing at Joe but had to duck as the gunfire from the shore raked their position.

Cloe fired a second behind Joe and knocked the man behind the machine gun to the deck in a spray of red mist. She shot three more of the men before they pointed toward the house. By now, there were two dozen AR15s, deer rifles, and one BAR peppering the deck with bullets. The ship lurched as the engine room reversed gear and backed toward the open ocean under full power.

Joe saw Cloe keep firing and killing the men on the deck as he sent another HE round into the side of the Bofors. Joe was shocked when the cannon turned toward him and fired. He held his breath as the round went high and wide over them. There was an explosion a block behind them as Joe shot again at the Bofors.

"Cloe, run!"

Joe ran down the roof, jumped the ten feet to the ground, and saw Cloe in midair as he fell. He saw her get up and run, so he took off behind her. They only ran a few yards until they heard an explosion and a second later a series of explosions coming from the direction of the river.

Joe stopped so suddenly he fell down in the sandy soil. "Cloe, I think the ship blew up. Follow me."

Joe led her to a house over a hundred yards away that had a good view of the river. They peered around the patio wall and saw the ship was several hundred yards out to sea and there was smoke rising from the deck and the Bofors was a tangled wreck.

"Damn, Cloe, I must have ruptured the next shell to be fed, and it blew the cannon to pieces when it set the other shells off."

Cloe was still breathing rapidly. "Dad, just tell me your story and I'll swear by it."

Joe swatted Cloe on the back of the head. "Girl, you're getting to be a smart ass just like your mom."

The ship was soon out of sight, and the local nurse patched Cobie and Charlie's wounds. Dan had a crew drive Joe's old Suburban back so Joe could take Cobie and Charlie back to the Fort in a large RV so they could rest. Joe drove all the way back even though Cloe insisted on driving. "Baby Girl, you can't drive a truck worth a hoot, and I'm not trusting you to drive this behemoth on these twisty assed curves. Go back and take a nap beside your husband."

Zeke and Joe changed their security protocols after that fiasco to include armed guards for Joe after almost having him captured and turned into a slave. Zeke considered Joe to be an essential leader and future founding father of their new nation.

☆

Chapter 18

Joe and Cobie reflected back on the past seven years over supper with Cloe, Charlie, and Charlie's parents, Jane and Ben. Joe was quiet for a while then spoke. I know we all think about Cole and wonder what happened to him. In my mind, he's somewhere around Virginia living a good life with a wife and a bunch of kids. I think that plane took Butch, the girls, and Cole to Washington, DC. Cole probably led a revolt and escaped along with the others. They are all living well and started a new country like we did."

Cloe laughed and nodded her head but down deep, she felt nothing but fear when she thought of what happened to Cole and the others.

They all traded stories until Joe mentioned his Dad and Mom. "I feel in my gut that Dad and Mom left the city, and they are living off the land in Tennessee. Dad was a lot like me in that he didn't have many survival skills but he knew how to hunt, fish, and trap. In my dreams, I think he has an old cabin on the Cumberland River outside of Nashville, and he hunkered down during the die off.

Hell, dad would be about 60 now, and Mom would be 62. I would love to go back there one day, but Zeke says it's still pretty rough east of the Mississippi River. One of our planes has flown that far east but was shot at several times. Zeke gave up on linking up with any of the new countries out east. I'd love for Dad to see our children and grandchildren. I miss my Dad."

Cloe wondered why Joe didn't miss his mom.

***

Joe had read the following letter several times a year in the last five years. In fact, he and his family read every one of the letters from his Grandma in order at least once a year and always found inspiration and humor in the dying thoughts of Joe's Grandma. Cobie teased Joe to no end about his Grandma's comments about him finding a woman. Everyone laughed their asses off when they heard the story about Joe's girlfriend and his best friend.

Joe lay in his hammock on the patio, read the letter one more time, and thanked God that his Grandma had been there for him and his family during the early years after the grid went down.

Dear Joe:

This is my last letter to you. Your damned Aunt is hovering over me like she gives a crap and she brought her worthless husband and kids to my house hoping that I would die today. I'm on oxygen and have a clear plastic tent over my head so it's a little tough writing plus I can't remember shit and keep writing the same thing several times.

I can laugh as I see the end coming because I know she ain't getting jack in my will.

If you get a chance, please make her life miserable. I don't ask for much as I lie here dying, but please stick it to her every time you get a chance. I talked with God, and he understands. He will be using you to start her Hell on Earth. Then he will turn her over to the devil to finish her sentence. Now I'd better get back to being Good Granny.

Joe if the shit hits the fan, I want you to promise me that you will go back to Tennessee to check on your dad when the dust settles. If Armageddon doesn't happen, just get your happy ass on a plane and fly home. Any who, go home and take your new woman with you to visit your dad and mom. (Boy, it's been two years. Even a monk would have found a good woman by now.) Try to get your Dad to go back to Oregon with you. If the SHTF hasn't happened, it will soon. You can count on it.

Joe, you are a good man, except for your Aunt, treat everyone with compassion that deserves it, and give the others what they deserve. Help others when you can but always take care of and protect your family.

Albert will be with me when I die so you don't have to say goodbye to him for me. Just tell him I still love him from the grave. Joe, I love you and hope that these letters have helped you get over your loss and maybe kept you sane as you started your new life up here in Oregon. Did I mention that I left a similar set of letters for your old man?

I will now say goodbye and best wishes for you and your new family. (Well, you should have one by now, anyway.)

Love Grandma

Joe laughed about the part about his Aunt. He had searched for her and her family but never found her. He finished the letter and went into his living room where his family traded stories about their adventures over the years. Joe rolled on the floor with his son and grandkids thinking he was the luckiest man on Earth.

☆

Epilog and Sample from my new series:

American Apocalypse EMP - Cole's Saga

Well, that was about the happiest ending I can imagine for a post-apocalyptic story. Joe, Cobie, Cloe, and Charlie lived long and prosperous lives. Cloe finally grew up, wasn't the drama queen of her youth, and became a great mother. Their friends prospered in their community and continued to improve Fort Earl.

They suffered pain and agony along the way as they rebuilt life in the great Northwest of the old USA. They eventually formed their own country and called it Jefferson. The new country stretched from the top half of California to Canada and over to the Dakota and Nebraska borders. Zeke was the first president and Bruce the first Vice President.

Joe, Cobie, Earl, Wes, Ben, Jane, and Dan were all considered to be some of the founding fathers and mothers of Jefferson.

They built a strong military to meet all threats and made the changes to the Federal Government that fixed the old problems of career politicians. No person could serve more than ten years total in any Federal Government capacity. They changed many of the laws that allowed corruption in government including the implementation of robust anti-corruption laws.

Many criminals and even the rogue FEMA troops tried to attack Jefferson and failed. The death penalty was used often and justly to rid the land of evil people. The country was much safer year to year, as the country of Jefferson's ideology spread south and east.

Now the only loose ends are whatever happened to Cole, Molly, and Joe's parents back in Tennessee. I intended to end the series without any possibility of a cliffhanger so I wouldn't hear that in ten reviews; however, as I scrambled to finish Cole and Molly's parts I kinda was carried away and kept writing past where they were planned to die at the hands of the slavers in Chico.

Therefore, you will see Cole, Joe's dad, Jack, and Molly star in a new series over in the Kentucky-Tennessee area. This would be a different series and have little to do with the crew out in Oregon, other than they are in Cole's past, and Joe's parents and Molly are in Cole's future.

Now I know some of you hardheaded readers might wonder if Grandma might show up in a future series. Of course, not, damn she died years ago; however, she wrote letters to Joe and remember she also wrote letters to Joe's dad.

What the heck happened to Joe's mom and dad and what are their names? I wrote these books and can't find their names. I just named them Jack and Helen because you will hear from them one day.

The first book in my next series has the working title "Cole's Saga." I'm scratching for a series title, and nothing grabs my fancy. The new spin-off series will have mention of Cole's family and girlfriend out in Oregon, but only in passing. This is a new series and tells the story of Cole and Jack's survival in the years after Cole was kidnapped and shipped to Kentucky. This series will be a different look at survival starting a year after the EMP blasts.

Mack Norman and I have to finish the Rogue's series this spring so I'll start on Cole's Saga after that series is complete.

Thanks for reading AMERICAN APOCALYPSE: RISING FROM THE DARKNESS the final novel in the series.

The End of the American Apocalypse series

Don't stop! Next is a sample from "Cole's Saga."

Thanks for reading my novel and please don't forget to give it a great review on Amazon. Remember to read my other books on Amazon.

AJ Newman

American Apocalypse "EMP"

Cole's Saga

Book 1

The next series starts with Joe Harp's father at the time the bombs first fell and then covers the year after the bombs fell. Then you get to find out how and when Cole and Jack's paths cross in 2039 a year after TSHTF. It will be a bit tricky with Jack back in 2038 and Cole moving forward in 2039 but we'll "Git er done."

Joe's father - Jack Harp. - SAMPLE

February 2038 Smyrna, Tennessee **Three days before TSHTF**

Joe's father, Jack Harp, was busy catching up from being off for his mom's funeral. His shop was in the middle of several large orders from a plastics factory. His Operations Manager had performed well during his weeklong absence for the funeral, but several customers needed attention due to a couple of late orders. The tool and die business was no different from any other. You had to do perfect work and deliver it on time. Jack soothed the customers and set up a golf outing for them and their wives down at the Robert Trent Jones Course in Muscle Shoals.

With that crisis handled, Jack slumped down in his chair and leaned back with his feet propped up on his desk. Then he saw the package his mom's lawyer had given him. "Shit, I forgot all about that. Mom would be pissed that I didn't open it the day I got it. "Carole, come here and bring me ..."

"I'm on the way," Carole, his administrative assistant yelled back to him.

Jack placed the package on his desk and stared at it while Carole poured them both three fingers of Pappy Van Winkle.

Jack had slumped down in his plush leather chair. "Damn, girl, you trying to get me drunk? It's only lunchtime."

Carole moved some paperwork and plopped her butt down on the edge of Jack's desk facing him with her barefoot on his leg. "Hon, it's been a long hard week with you gone and your Ops Manager tried getting in my panties three times. I'm tired, pissed off, and earned this drink. You can fire me or give me that raise you promised. Right now I don't give a rat's ass which you do."

Carole was ten years younger than Jack and a real spitfire. She kept him on schedule, was the receptionist, and handled the purchase orders. She was his right-armed woman in the office, and everyone knew she was damned good at her job. Carole had flirted with Jack for the last six of the seven years she worked for him. Jack was loyal to his wife, Helen, and never cheated on her. He was old fashioned even though he was sure that wasn't true on Helen's part. He was guilty of lusting in his heart for Carole but not in deed. He enjoyed the teasing and flirting but always stopped before it got too dangerous.

Jack raised his glass for a toast. "Carole you are the one constant bright spot in my life. I hope like hell that you have a bright spot in yours. We'll talk about that raise next week when I am caught up. Oh, did that hound dog Larry get in your panties?"

Carole tossed her head back, fluffed her hair, and then rubbed her shoeless foot on Jack's leg. "No, he tried awful hard, but you know Jack, I'm saving myself for you."

The blood rushed to Jack's face. "Carole, we've been here before and you know I won't cheat on Helen."

"Hon, I wouldn't have you if you cheated on Helen. I want you to dump her cheating ass and marry me. Why don't you ask her why she meets Larry on Wednesdays when you play golf with our clients? Ask her about the Swartz account and the funny accounting. Larry is also bonking your bookkeeper."

This made Jack's blood boil, but he didn't take the bait. "Carole, I have to check out this box my Mom left me. So would you take your gorgeous ass back to your desk before everyone in the company thinks I'm banging you on my desk?"

Carole stood up and bent down to give Jack a kiss on the forehead. "Hon, they have thought that for five years. You have no idea what you are missing, and I'm about to give up trying to get you to chase me."

Jack poured himself another stiff drink and opened the box to see a letter on top.

Dear Jack:

Son, you know I died from my cancer, and I hope you and Joe gave me a decent funeral. What you didn't know was that I wrote you and Joe a bunch of letters before I died. I started writing Joe's letters when I knew the end was near about five or six months ago. I filled them with wisdom and survival hints because I really believe the shit will hit the fan soon. I know your Helen thinks I'm full of shit but just listen to the news.

I wrote the letters to Joe to help him with my wisdom when I realized that you and I had grown apart over the years. I feel you could also use a bit of my wisdom. I wrote and rewrote this letter several times over the past few months and just finished it again the day after what's her face was crushed in Joe's truck while screwing that so-called friend of his.

Jack, your wife, is out spreading her charms around the town. I think you know this, but just in case I have to tell you something, that will make you mad at me. I hired a private investigator out of Nashville, and he came back with a basket full of juicy crap on Helen. The list of men she is screwing is the size of a small phone book. That's not the bad part. She and Your Operations Manager have been stealing from you for many years. Kick her sorry ass out. The details and pictures are at the bottom of the box. Ugly stuff.

I know it's not fair for you to see this after I'm dead, but I knew we would just fight and you would tell me to mind my own damned business. I love you Jack and want the best for you. The only thing Helen ever did good for you was to give you your son Joe. I love that boy as much as I love you.

Okay, now I need to tell you about the rest of the contents. There are over 130 letters in this box. There are instructions on each bundle. Read them in order. They will help you deal with Helen and might help you to survive if you start prepping now.

I love you and goodbye from my earthly body.

Love Mom

Jack downed the drink. "Oh, Carole come here with your notepad and please bring the Swartz account."

He heard her scramble opening the filing cabinet. Carole then entered the room. "Hon, it's about time you took my advice."

He motioned her to sit down on the edge of his desk, took her shoe off, and placed her foot on his leg. "Carole, I need your help. Get me the paperwork ready for my signature to give you a $10,000 raise per year when we are done. Now take some notes - Hire a PI to check up on Larry and Helen. Fire Sally, our bookkeeper. Hire a forensic accountant to check our books. Find the best divorce lawyer in Nashville. Get a realtor to find me a cabin on Lake Barkley or Kentucky Lake.

Purchase a bunch of prepper shit. Take Carole out to dinner and bang ...err ... make love to her."

Carole was stunned. "Jack, are you sure? I've been chasing you so long I never thought that you'd catch me. I'll get all of the others in motion ASAP, but you need to think about that last thing for a while before acting. Don't fall for me because your wife is a piece of crap."

"Carole, don't argue with the boss. The news today is terrible. The president thinks we are going to be attacked if we don't strike first. The Chinese hacked Japan and EU banking systems and erased most of the financial data. The world is going to hell, and you are my only bright spot. I have thought about you, day and night for five years. If the world ends tomorrow, I want you to be by my side," Jack said very tenderly.

Carole slid onto Jacks lap, and they embraced.

Jack didn't worry about his cheating wife but couldn't get Joe off his mind. He planned to call Joe the next day but the shit hit the fan, and all he could do was try to make sure he and Carole survived. He would think about his son many times over the next year.

Jack started prepping too late to do much good. He had three days to prepare for the end of the world. The missiles exploded three days later, and the grid was down. What would Jack do to survive? Would he survive?

***

Cole Biggs – Digging Coal - SAMPLE

2039 – One year after TSHTF

Cole woke up with his head on Molly's lap. "Where are we? What happened to my head? Did I get kicked by a mule?"

Molly lowered her gaze. "Cole, thank God you came to. The plane is landing, and they will kill you if you can't work in the coal mines. You saved us, and the slavers hit you on the head. You are lucky they didn't kill you for pointing your gun at them."

Cole looked up into Molly's deep green eyes and felt her red hair on his face. "I remember you. We were taking you and your cousins to live in our community. I thought we killed all of the slavers."

Molly stared down at the ruggedly handsome young man. "No, I think my dad said they are very well organized and are spread out all over the country. They supply workers for the FEMA farms, factories, and mines. I told them you were my husband to try to keep us all together. We have a couple of more stops, but they plan to take us to Western Kentucky so you can work in a mine and we can work on a farm. Oh, what is your last name?"

Cole's mind was overworked, but a grin came over his face. "So, Mrs. Biggs, I have a beautiful wife, but I'm a slave that is to spend the rest of his short life slaving in a coal mine."

"The wife part is just a ruse. Don't get any ideas, Mr. Biggs" she tersely replied.

"Hey, where is my friend Butch?"

Molly looked away. "I'm sorry, but I'm fairly certain they killed him during the attack. He would be with us if he were still alive. I'm sorry for your loss."

A frown came over Cole's face as he remembered that Molly's mom and dad had been working with the gangs and slavers to provide men, women, and children to the slavers. There was no indication that Molly or her cousins knew of the involvement, but Cole didn't trust her and would keep a sharp eye on her and her cousins.

Cole replayed the last year over in his mind, and even though it was filled with death, destruction, and heartache, it was the best year of his life. He had met his mentors, Joe and Earl, his mom married a great man, Ben, and he fell in love with Cloe. Even though Cloe was too young for him, he still cared for her and missed her. Not saying goodbye to these people that meant so much to him was horrible. He was confident they all thought he was dead.

Molly saw the lady guard rise up from her seat and walk toward her. The lady stopped and nudged Cole with her toe. "Is he alive? If not he gets pitched from the plane now."
Cole tapped the woman on the leg. "Ma'am I'm still kicking and ready for duty. I just need some aspirin for this headache, and I'm good to go."
The woman nudged Cole with her toe again. "It would be a shame to kick such a handsome young man from the plane when we have so many coal mines and factories that need your strong back. Girl, get used to your man coming home stinking

of coal with black dust covering him from head to toe and only able to bathe once a week."

That evening they landed at Muhlenberg County airport close to Powderly, Kentucky. A man in a black uniform met the plane. "Families to the right and everyone else to the left. Families get on the blue bus. The others get on the yellow bus. You are being taken to your new home courtesy of the New United States of America. You will be fed, clothed, and kept safe by our new government. Your days of starving and fear are over. You will be expected to work hard to help us rebuild our country. Women will work in the factories and farms. Men will work in the coal mines. We only have a few machines working so most of the mining is manual labor. Get on the busses."

It was only a few miles to Graham, Kentucky to the old abandoned Dyno Nobel arms factories off Highway 175. The factory had manufactured missiles and bombs for the US Military years ago, but the buildings were in good shape, and several had been converted to dormitories and living units for families. The bus stopped in front of a large rambling building. An older woman told them to separate into family groups. "Okay, you two go in the door and go to apartment number 8." She looked at her clipboard when she saw Cole's group had four adults. "What's the deal here? Mister, do you have three wives?"
Cole looked down at the woman's feet. "No ma'am, Molly is my wife, and the twins are her sisters. We were captured out in Oregon and brought here."
"You were rescued from the apocalypse mister," the woman shouted.
Cole solemnly apologized. "Sorry, ma'am. We are very grateful to you and the New United States of America for delivering us from the apocalypse. We will work hard for you."
The woman liked the kiss ass response. "Take your family in that door and up the stairs to apartment 3A. It will be tight, but if you're not shy you will all get along just fine."

226

Before Cole could take a step, a black bus drove up, and a man yelled for him to get on the bus. "Climb aboard. This is the night shift bus to the number 5 Utopia Mine. Be here every evening at 7:00 pm sharp. If you miss your bus, you will be punished."

Molly quickly hugged Cole and kissed him goodbye. "Cole, we need to act like we care for each other out in public."

Cole walked away to the bus and looked back at Molly before stepping on the bus steps. She waved and then turned to go into the apartment complex. The driver took off before Cole could sit down, which caused him to trip and fall on the floor. A large man stuck a massive hand out. "Son, you look like you need a hand up."

Cole took the man's hand, pulled himself up, and sat down next to him. There was barely room in the seat for both of them.

"I'm Deacon Brown, and I'm glad to meet you."

"Hello, I'm Cole Biggs, and I'm glad to meet you also. Hey, wasn't there a Deacon Brown who played defensive tackle for the Kentucky Racers a while back?"

The large black man grinned a big toothy smile. "That's me. I was a rich spoiled football player, and now I use a pick and shovel in a mine. I was driving from Nashville to Louisville when the bombs fell and found myself in a FEMA camp. The camp was better than throwing rocks at rabbits for supper until I found out that these people didn't know that Lincoln freed the slaves. What's your story?"

Cole took a deep breath and sighed. "Would you believe that yesterday I was out in Oregon hunting slavers and killing them?"

"No you're shitting me, aren't you?"

"Nope, no shitting."

THANKS FOR READING THIS SAMPLE OF "COLE'S SAGA" FROM MY NEXT SERIES.

Remember to push the **Follow** button below the author's photo on Amazon to follow AJ Newman and get notice of new books.

All novels contain some errors. If you find an error, please send a note with the error to the author at ajnewman123@yahoo.com

If you like my novel, please post a review on Amazon. @ http://www.amazon.com/-/e/B00HT84V6U

To contact or follow the Author, please leave comments @:
https://www.facebook.com/newmananthonyj/

To view other books by AJ Newman, go to Amazon to my Author's page:
http://www.amazon.com/-/e/B00HT84V6U

A list of my other books follows at the end.

Thanks,   A.J. Newman

BOOKS BY MY GOOD FRIEND CLIFF DEANE

Vigilante Series

Into The Darkness   Into the Fray

Pale Horse   No Quarter

The Way West   Indian Territory

RED ALERT: MISSILES INBOUND: The OORT Chronicles

Virus: Strain of Islam (with AJ Newman)

Cliff's books are available on Amazon @

https://www.amazon.com/Cliff-Deane/e/B06XGPG7YZ/ref=sr_tc_2_0?qid=1514742671&sr=1-2-ent

Cliff Deane's Amazon page

https://www.amazon.com/Cliff-Deane/e/B06XGPG7YZ/ref=sr_tc_2_0?qid=1514742671&sr=1-2-ent

VIGILANTE: INTO THE DARKNESS pulls no punches when it comes to the horrific details of a worldwide grid down situation, from the effect on the food chain from ants to rats. With so many dead, how do the survivors deal with rotting corpses, diseases, and villains? Will good triumph over evil? Maybe...

Levins retires from the Army and is off on vacation before starting his new job. He suffers a horrendous loss accompanying "lights out" and must find a way to help humanity to keep his own sanity.

He has no bug out bag, no hidden weapons cache, no transportation, and no Cabin in the woods capable of launching a satellite. What does he do, and how does he do it? Levi will walk us through his path to survival. Perhaps it may one day be yours...

Vigilante: Into the Darkness takes us on a journey to try to stave off the New Dark Age brought on by a worldwide EMP apocalypse.
Can Government survive when no food is being trucked to the masses? Can our military survive without the tons of food needed each and every meal? The answers are here.

AJ Newman

*

Books by AJ Newman

American Apocalypse"EMP"
Cole's Saga (summer 2018)

American Apocalypse
American Survivor
Descent Into Darkness
Reign of Darkness
Rising from the Apocalypse

Alien Apocalypse
The Virus
Surviving

A Family's Apocalypse Series
Cities on Fire
Family Survival

After the Solar Flare
Alone in the Apocalypse
Adventures in the Apocalypse

The Day America Died Murder Mystery
New Beginnings
Old Enemies
Frozen Apocalypse

A Samantha Jones

Where the Girls Are Buried
Who Killed the Girls?

The Adventures of John Harris Norman
Surviving
Hell in the Homeland
Tyranny in the Homeland
Revenge in the Homeland
Apocalypse in the Homeland
John Returns
Deane
of Islam

AJ Newman and Mack

Rogues Origin
Rogues Rising
Rogues Journey
Rogues Rebellion (Summer 2018)

AJ Newman and Cliff

Terror in the USA: Virus: Strain

These books are available on Amazon: AJ Newman – Amazon Page

To contact the Author, please leave comments @:www.facebook.com/newmananthonyj

About the Author

AJ Newman is the author of 24 science fiction and mystery novels that have been published on Amazon. He was born and raised in a small town in the western part of Kentucky. His Dad taught him how to handle guns very early in life, and he and his best friend Mike spent summers shooting .22 rifles and fishing.

Reading is his passion, and he read every book he could get his hands on and fell in love with science fiction. He graduated from USI with a degree in Chemistry and made a career working in manufacturing and logistics, but always fancied himself as an author.

He served six years in the Army National Guard in an armored unit and spent six years performing every function on M48 and M60 army tanks. This gave him great respect for our veterans who lay their lives on the line to protect our country and freedoms.

He currently resides in a small town just outside of Owensboro, Kentucky with his wife Patsy and their four tiny Shih Tzu's, Sammy, Cotton, Callie, and Benny. All except Benny are rescue dogs.

Made in the USA
Las Vegas, NV
04 August 2022

52706513R00135